D0720544

# STONE RAGE

### A Stone Cold Thriller

## J. D. WESTON

## STRIKE ONE

"WHAT THE HELL ARE WE DOING OUT HERE, LES?"

"This is where the boss said to meet them."

"It's pitch black, mate, I can't see anything. There could be fifty of them out there."

"Stop being paranoid," said Les. "Not like you to be jumpy."

"I'm not jumpy. I just don't trust them, the dirty, sly little-"

"We'll be out of here before you know it," replied Les. "Chill out. I used to bring the birds over here."

"Over here? What for? This place gives me the creeps. Can we at least have the heater on? It's freezing."

"Why do *think* I brought them here?" said Les, turning up the Jaguar's temperature dial. "A bit of rough and tumble, Jay, they loved it."

"Is that what they told you? How many of them came back for a second night of creepy love in the freaky field?"

"Not many," laughed Les. "Well, one actually, a few times. Sticky Sarah, we used to call her. She used to like that people could see in, dirty cow, voyeurism I think they call that."

"Sticky Sarah?"

"Yeah, strange girl she was, had a great set but she was a bit weird."

"Les, nothing about what you just said is normal. Firstly, why was she called Sticky Sarah?"

"Well, it was more like tacky really. But the name Tacky Sarah didn't work."

"Oh right, and when you say 'we,' can I assume that you weren't the only one to experience Sticky Sarah's tacky sensation?"

"No, we all had a go. Well, most of us, apart from Little Lee, poor fella was a slow developer. I have no idea how that guy survived childhood, he's probably still a virgin now."

"And when you say that Sticky Sarah used to enjoy being watched, do you mean to say that you brought her over here and banged her in the back of your car so other blokes could see in?"

"Yeah, dog walkers and stuff, she loved it," said Les.

"Did that not ever strike you as a bit weird, Les?"

"Not really."

Jay looked away from him in disgust. "I can't see shit out there," he muttered. "What was it anyway?"

"What was what?"

"The car, what car did you have?"

"Well, you know, I was young, didn't have enough money for my own car."

"Don't tell me you used your mum's car to smash Sticky Sarah around and have a load of dirty pervs stand around."

"No, no, no, I never," said Les. "I have got some decency."

"So, whose car was it?"

"I don't bloody know, do I?"

"You nicked it?"

"Yeah, of course I did. Had a different one each week. I learned to drive in a nicked motor, my old man taught me."

"You what?" said Jay. "Your old man taught you to drive in a stolen car?"

"Yeah, he didn't know it was stolen, I told him I'd borrowed it off a mate."

"What if he got caught? How would you explain that?"

"Behave, Jay, I was fifteen years old. I didn't know any better."

"You're something else, you know that?"

Les laughed. "It's been a good old life, Jay. Had some great times I have."

"Don't get all teary on me now."

"No, you know what I mean. Don't you ever wonder?"

"Wonder what?"

"You know, if you died, have you done all the things you wanted to do?"

"I done most of them, Les," said Jay. "There's a few things still on the list though. One day I'll get around to ticking them off."

"What's that then?"

"Well, I might see if Sticky Sarah is still around and see if she fancies a bunk up while some old perv knocks one out."

Both side windows exploded in the car, sending glass all over the two men. Big hands reached in and dragged them through the car windows. Les pulled a knife and slashed blindly at the huge men who pinned him down on the grass. One of the men, a bald man with tattoos on his face, held Les' throat tightly and the other stopped his knife hand waving around by standing on his arm. A large knee came down onto Les' chest and, one by one, each of the fingers that held the knife were wrenched up, bent backwards and broken.

Les screamed in pain. He struggled, but it was useless against the size and weight of the man on top of him. Eventually, the last finger was snapped back like a twig, and the knife was taken from him.

The smaller of the two bald men that pinned him down held the knife curiously. He turned it in his hands, put the point in Les' eye, and slowly pushed down until the blade entered Les' brain and he fell silent.

Jay was on the other side of the car. Strong arms held him against the Jaguar's sleek paintwork. No words were spoken. Jay stopped struggling.

A tall, willowy man in a long overcoat stepped from the darkness into the pale moonlight. Jay could barely make out the features of his face but saw the glint of a scar that ran from the man's eye to his mouth, through his lips and down his chin to his throat.

The man gave a gesture to his men, who stood beside Les' body, to open the car boot. Opening it, they removed the sports holdall that contained four kilos of cocaine. They checked it and returned the nod to the boss.

Jay stared up at the man and spat.

"You will take a message to your boss."

"Fuck you, send a letter."

One of the men holding Jay landed a huge fist on his nose. Jay felt the bone break and tasted blood almost immediately.

"I am a reasonable man, but I am a businessman. It seems like your boss and I are in the same business. Competition."

"So run a sale or something. Isn't that what businessmen do?"

"It's an option," the man replied. "But I prefer not to cut profits for the sake of a few easy sales. I prefer to cut the competition." The man reached inside his coat and pulled out a long fillet knife. He flexed the blade and ran his finger along the thin steel.

"You will deliver the message for me?" asked the man.

"I'll tell him some ugly bloke from some shit stink part of

Europe wants his balls cut off," said Jay. "How does that sound, wanker?"

"Hold him," the man said calmly.

The two men either side of Jay grabbed his hair and held him tight. The man in the coat stepped forward and ran the side of the blade across Jay's nose. With one hand, he pulled Jay's ear out from his head, and with the other, he sliced through the tissue and gristle in two neat, clean slices. Jay screamed and struggled against the two much larger men, but couldn't move. Spit flew from his gritted teeth, and his eyes were clamped shut as he fought the searing pain. He felt the man pull on his other ear, dull and hard. He felt the blade touch his skin sharply. Then he felt nothing but the burn of where his ears once were.

"Make sure he doesn't lose those, he may need them one day," said the man in the coat, as he wiped the blood from the blade onto Jay's jacket.

Jay's knees had given way, but his weight was easily supported by the two men. They dropped him to the ground face first, then kicked him to roll him over. Jay pulled his hands to his head, but his wounds were too tender to touch. Blood had run across his face into his eyes. He felt his arms being tugged outwards then felt a sharp point in the palm of his hand. He glared helplessly through the sticky blood to see one of the large men with a cordless drill. Then he felt the screw tear through his tendons, fixing an ear to his open hand with a long, gold screw.

## THE WOLFPACK

A LIGHT RAIN FELL LIKE MIST IN THE FOREST WHERE Harvey Stone took his early morning run. His mind was clear, and his body had healed from the beating it had taken during the last job he and his team had worked.

The mission had been their hardest yet and had cost the team dearly. They'd lost Denver, their driver, during the investigation, and each of the team were healing in their own way. The physical scars of battle often heal quicker than the mental scars, he thought.

Harvey leapt over an old fallen log, which he remembered from a run he had taken a few weeks previously. He never ran the same route twice, but often the crisscrossing paths intertwined in the deepest areas of Epping Forest, the forest that lay behind his house.

He ran with boots on for ankle support, and to make the challenge harder. Harvey didn't believe in running with bricks in a bag, but when he did run, he gave everything he had. Running with bricks in a rucksack was a military approach to training, and Harvey thought it doubtlessly worked, but would also cripple a man over time. Harvey wasn't a military man or even ex-military. He sat at the other end of that vocational spectrum, not quite as far along as the terrorists he had recently fought, but definitely on the wrong end.

Harvey had been raised by the leader of a well-known crime family, John Cartwright. John had fostered Harvey and his sister when they were young after their parents had apparently committed double suicide. Harvey had never believed the story of his parents' death and actively pursued the truth.

When Harvey had been twelve and Hannah, his sister, had been a few years older, he had witnessed her being raped, which led to her suicide.

The emotional damage the small boy Harvey took on changed his life forever. He fell under the wing of John Cartwright's minder who taught him how to channel his aggression, how to defend himself, and eventually, how to kill.

Three men had raped Hannah. The first man had been Harvey's first kill. It took a further twenty years for him to find the other two men, and deliver their own retribution. That was when Harvey had removed himself from the circles of crime that sheltered him, and stepped tentatively across the line into the world of crime fighting. Harvey took that step armed with memories he'd rather not have and a list of people he needed to kill.

The list had two names. It was short, but it was a list that guided Harvey.

Harvey had been given two options after killing one of his sister's rapists, who he'd boiled alive in a copper bathtub until his internal organs had eventually cooked and his heart had stopped. The first option was prison, where he would likely serve the rest of his life and lose any opportunity to finish the list.

The second option had been to work with Frank Carver and his small team, which focused solely on fighting organised crime.

The choice had been simple, stay out of prison and work the list. Finding his sister's rapists had been therapeutic, cleansing and, above all, motivating. His list then focused on the mystery of his parents, who killed them and why, and his best friend and mentor, Julios, who had been shot by an unknown man. Then, during the last job, Harvey discovered that Julios had been to one to kill his parents. Harvey had been hit hard by the news. He'd been betrayed all his life. But the image of Julios standing over his parents' bodies had desecrated Harvey's earliest memories, memories of Julios training him, guiding him and sculpturing Harvey into the stone-cold killer he had become.

The list was nearly empty. He still hadn't discovered Julios' killer, but that was no longer a priority. Harvey had grown, he'd become part of the team, and had come to love his colleagues, something he never thought possible. He would find out how and why Julios had killed his parents, someday. But, for now, he was at peace. Frank Carver had removed the noose from Harvey's neck and set him free. Prison no longer loomed in the background; Harvey had paid his penance. Faced with the choice to stay working with his team, or to remove himself from everything tying him to the criminal world and live out his days in a small cottage in the south of France, Harvey had decided to stay.

He enjoyed the activity. He enjoyed the team and the banter and positivity that came from taking down gangs or stopping a tragedy. Harvey was healing in his own way, not from the wounds, mental or physical, that came from battle, but from the damage he had caused in his earlier life as a hitman for John Cartwright. The lives he'd torn apart so that John could grow richer. The fathers, brothers, and sons he had taken from daughters, sisters and mothers. He could never give those lives back, but with his remaining time on the planet, Harvey could do some good. He could make a difference.

The trees opened up as the forest grew thinner at the edge, where the houses and roads ruled the landscape. The last obstacle was a steep hill, covered with a carpet of leaves and twigs. Harvey opened himself up and attacked the hill full speed, lifting his legs high, planting his feet hard and pushing his body up. His breaths came in short rhythmic bursts, and his arms pumped with each stroke. He broke the crest of the hill and jogged to the road, where he walked back to his house, breathing and stretching, and warming down.

Harvey leaned with his hands high on the shower wall and let the hot water run over him. He turned the water temperature up until it stung his skin then let his body get used to the heat before turning it up more. It was his morning shower routine. Within a few minutes, the shower was on full heat, and steam filled the bathroom. Then he turned the heat to cold, fast, removing the hot and replacing it with freezing cold water. His body tensed and grew red as the blood surged to the outer layers of skin to protect it.

He pulled a towel from the hook and walked to his bedroom. As usual, he dressed before drying properly, wearing a plain white t-shirt, black cargo pants and tan boots. Pulling the leather biker's jacket over his shirt, Harvey walked past the mirror without so much as a glance. He stuffed his Sig Sauer in his waistband and performed his routine of leaving the house. Every window was checked, and every door. He then took a mental snapshot of the rooms before leaving. Harvey had been trained to see if anything had been moved. Everything had a place, symmetrical, and easy to spot if he'd had an intrusion or something was disturbed.

Harvey used the interior door to his garage and locked it behind him. His motorbike helmet hung from a single hook on the wall in its protective black nylon bag. He pulled it off and hung the bag back up then started the BMW's engine. The garage door was operated from a small fob in his pocket. He rolled out, closed the garage behind him and pulled out onto the road.

Harvey rode slowly, enjoying the cool morning and minding the small puddles that had collected on the side of the roads.

It wasn't until he entered the M11 motorway southbound that he pulled his visor down and opened up the throttle. Less than twenty-five minutes later, he pulled up outside his colleague's apartment. He left the engine running, and lowered his boots to the ground, balancing the weight of the bike between his thighs.

Melody Mills led the team's operations; she made the plans. Guided by the team in their individual fields of expertise, she called the shots and reported to Frank. Melody stepped from the plush apartment block in long black boots, tight black leggings and a short leather jacket. She swept her long black hair over one shoulder and pulled on a helmet.

Harvey stood and held the bike upright as she swung her leg over behind him.

"Morning, Harvey." She gave him a firm squeeze to let him know she was comfortable and he pulled off. The team's headquarters was a short ride from the Docklands, situated beside the Thames Barrier in Silvertown. As Harvey pulled onto the North Woolwich Road, he slowed then stopped to one side.

"What's up?" asked Melody.

Harvey was looking across the busy road at a burnt out pub. Acrid smoke still hung in the morning air.

Melody followed his gaze. "Oh that, yeah that was on fire when I came home last night. It's a rough pub apparently, never went in there," said Melody.

"You know who ran it?" asked Harvey, raising the visor on his helmet.

"Haven't a clue," said Melody.

"For someone who works in organised crime, you don't know much, do you?" he jibed.

"Why?" said Melody defensively.

"That pub and the bookies next door was run by Carnell," said Harvey. "I hope for someone's sake that it was an accident, but I doubt it somehow."

"Carnell?" asked Melody. "Bobby Bones?"

"Don't ever let him hear you call him that."

"Why is he called that?"

"The only people that ever called him that, called him it once, then never called him nothing ever again. Or anyone else for that matter."

"You ever run into him?" asked Melody.

"Once or twice. He doesn't know me, but yeah, I had a run in with a few of his guys once, a long time ago. Apparently, he's a decent guy, but you only cross the line once."

"I didn't even know he had pubs. Last we heard of him his boys did a cash transit over, they went away, and he didn't even show up for court."

"Yeah, that was last you heard of him, but that doesn't mean he's been quiet. He's a lively one. John Cartwright pushed him out of East Ham and Plaistow, and he ventured further into town. I know he's got a few bookies under his wing too. I'd have money that fire was a hit, and he's not the sort of guy to take it lying down."

"Who'd hit him?"

"No-one this side of the water. He's a madman," said Harvey. "Let's go. Best not be seen staring at the charred remains of Bobby Bones' pub."

Harvey started the bike.

"I thought you said not to call him that?" said Melody.

"I said for *you* not to let *him* hear *you* call him that," replied Harvey. "*I'll* call him what I like." Harvey gave Melody a little wink in the mirror, lowered his visor, and pulled away hard. He felt Melody's hands dig into his sides as she held on tight.

―――――――

Harvey pulled into the headquarters and parked his bike in its spot beside the team's new VW van and the Audi saloon. He killed the engine, waited for Melody to climb off, then kicked the stand down, and climbed off himself, putting his helmet in the bike's back box.

Reg wasn't at his computer and Jackson, the team's new driver and engineer, was nowhere to be seen.

"Up here," called Frank from the mezzanine floor that ran the length of the right-hand wall. The mezzanine was home to Frank's office, a meeting room that was never used, and a break room where the team could eat, which was used as a meeting room.

Harvey and Melody joined the rest of the team in the meeting room, and Melody poured a coffee from the pot before sitting down.

"We ready?" asked Frank.

"Sure," said Melody. "I suddenly feel like we're late. Did we forget something?"

"No," said Frank, "but there have been some developments that we need to discuss."

"Great, a new case," said Melody.

"I like your enthusiasm, Mills. However, I'm not so sure you'll be as enthused when you hear about this one," said Frank.

He turned and faced the room, looking serious. "Are we all familiar with the Albanian mob?"

"Not on a first name basis, sir," said Reg. "But I'm pretty sure we all know what they're up to."

"What are they up to, Tenant?"

"Hookers, coke, and protection, isn't it, sir?"

"Right, illegal prostitution, selling drugs and extortion," said Frank. "We've known about them for a long while, but you know as well as I do that unless we hit the main man, making arrests isn't going to stop the problem. We're better off concentrating our efforts elsewhere, somewhere we can make a difference."

"So do we have enough on him, the main man now?" asked Melody. "Is that what this is about?"

"No, Melody, we don't unfortunately."

"So why the change?"

"Well, every now and then, the types of gangs we're talking about, not just Albanians but home-grown gangs too, will feel the need to stretch their legs, push boundaries and remind the firm next door that they are around, usually in the form of a little turf war." Frank hit the space bar on his laptop, which was connected to a large TV. An image of a dead man with a knife in his eye came up on the screen.

"Ohhh," said Reg. "He didn't see that coming."

"He probably did, Tenant," said Frank. "That's a nasty way to go."

Frank hit the right arrow on the laptop's keyboard. An image of a man with his ears removed from his head and screwed to his hands appeared.

"See no evil, hear no evil?" asked Reg.

"No, it's not some intelligent criminal mastermind playing games and leaving clues," said Frank. "I almost wish it was." He closed the image on the screen and returned his attention to his team. "This is the work of the Albanian mob. The men you see here are members of local firms, wanted for petty crimes, and on the watch list of the drug squad who are waiting for the big one to put them away."

"They weren't watching very hard, were they?" said Reg.

"Do you know how many individuals are on the watch list of the drug squad?"

"Yeah, I get it, loads."

"So what's the point of all this then?" said Harvey. "Where are you going?"

"Ah, Stone, a timely introduction. I'll answer your question in just a minute. But first I want to show you another photo or two."

Frank opened a photo from his desktop. It showed a row of shops totally burnt out. An ambulance was on the scene, and uniformed policemen stood outside to stop the public entering.

"I'm guessing that wasn't caused by a cigarette?" said Jackson.

"You're right," said Frank. "It wasn't a cigarette. See these flats here, above the shops?" The team nodded. "Who do you think lived in these flats?"

"Albanians?"

"No, Tenant, wrong. Ordinary people lived in those flats. Two office workers, a single mum with two small babies, twins in fact. A young couple due to get married." Frank paused and took the time to connect with his team individually. "They all died. Seven bodies, two of them less than a year old."

The room was silent as they all took the news in.

"Sad, isn't it?" said Frank.

"Who started the fire, sir?" asked Melody.

"A local firm started the fire, Mills. Killed their own, if you want to put it that way. According to the fire report, the cab firm downstairs was doused in petrol, as were the cars outside that belonged to the cab firm, and of course the firm belonged to our friends, the Albanians."

"So it's the local boys against the Albanians, is it?"

"So who exactly are *we* going after?" asked Harvey.

Frank took a deep breath and let it out slowly and audibly. "Both. This will be a long operation. We don't have access to the right people yet. But when we do, we'll be taking down the local firm and the Albanians, no prejudice. It will be messy, and we will be working with other teams to accomplish this."

"Carnell?" asked Harvey.

Frank looked at Harvey with raised eyebrows, questioning his comment. "No, Harvey, actually it's not, not according to the reports from the drug squad anyway. But what makes you say that?"

"His pub and his bookies up the road got burned down last night. We saw it this morning."

"Interesting, but hopefully unrelated."

"Something tells me it's not as unrelated as you hope," said Harvey. "Who's the local firm you think started the fire?"

"We don't know who's running it, yet," said Frank. "But they're smart, and they're tooled up, judging by the mess they've been making of the Albanians. The war is getting out of hand. Our job is to stop it, to prevent more innocent people dying and put an end to the mindless violence that has grown from the occasional dead thug winding up in the street to where we are now, with daily occurrences of violence and bodies."

"What's your plan, sir?" asked Melody.

"Well, first of all, we need to know who's running the local firm. Would you agree with that, Stone?"

Harvey didn't reply. He didn't need to. Harvey had learned from his mentor, Julios, at an early age how to communicate without words. Gestures, expressions, stares.

He often found them to be more powerful than words them-selves and allowed him to continue with his stream of thoughts without breaking into conversation.

"Then," said Frank, "we need to get involved."

"Get involved, sir?" asked Reg.

"He means go in undercover," said Harvey.

"What, all of us?" asked Reg.

"No, Reg," said Harvey. "Just me."

---

"You'll have an implant, a chip inserted under your skin so we can see where you are at all times," said Frank.

"No wires," said Harvey. "Too risky."

"Agreed," said Frank. "But we'll schedule regular meet-ings. I want a full briefing every day, and I want to see a legend before you do anything."

"A legend?"

"A profile; your name, what you do for a living, where you were born. You need to commit these details to memory. You'll be infiltrating some serious players, and if they catch wind that you're not who you say you are, you'll be torn apart."

"Do we have an in?"

"I was hoping you'd be able-"

"You was hoping to use my criminal past to get in?" said Harvey. "You do realise this is a rival gang to the firm I worked with, and there's a good chance I've done jobs on them already? You don't even know who the boss is yet."

"Are you known to them?" asked Frank.

"Only by name. I doubt anyone would know what I look like. I did a pretty good job of staying downwind. I wasn't a face."

"Any ideas on how we can get in?"

"Yeah, I've got an idea," said Harvey. "Bobby Bones."

"Carnell?" said Frank. "He's not involved."

"Yeah he is, you just don't know it," said Harvey. "Listen, someone burned down his pub last night. Now that someone either is seriously stupid or is prodding for a retaliation."

"So you're going to get in with Carnell?"

"Not *in* as such, but close enough to paint us a picture," said Harvey. "He's got another pub down the road, and if that one isn't burned down as well, I'll go for a pint. But there is one thing."

"What?"

"He's a bastard, Frank."

"Carnell?"

"Yeah, if it comes on top, I'm taking no chances. I'll be carrying, and I'll shoot my way out. If he realises I'm with the police in any way shape or form, he'll skin me alive."

"Is that why they call him Bobby Bones?" asked Reg.

"Why don't you ask him, Reg?" replied Harvey. "I hear he loves to sit down and tell people about where he got the nickname."

"Tell us a story, Harvey," said Reg. "Tell us about Bobby 'Bones' Carnell and how he got his name."

Harvey looked across at Frank who rested on the table at the head of the room and nodded.

"Well, Reg," began Harvey, "rumour has it that when Bobby was a lad, some boys were picking on him. So he waited until he got one alone, beat him up and cut the boy's finger off."

"That's not so bad, considering what we deal with here," said Reg.

"He was about ten years old, Reg," continued Harvey. "Then, a few weeks later he got another one alone, and he did the same thing, and then again with the last one. None of the three boys talked. They all told their parents they had accidents. Not one person pointed at Bobby, excuse the pun." Harvey pushed off the wall he'd been leaning on and walked to the centre of the room. "Bobby was left alone after that until he hit mid-teens, and he got into an older crew, did some robberies and got caught. Oddly enough, the witness that was going to testify lost all her fingers."

"Her?" said Melody. "He cut off a *woman's* fingers?"

"Yeah, some woman suddenly forgot what she saw and didn't stand up. Carnell walked free. It wasn't until he'd matured into doing bank jobs and running protection rackets that his fetish really took hold though. A rival gang, I forget the name, with a couple of heavies, came onto his turf, did a few of his blokes over. Bobby had them tied up in the butcher shop next door to his local pub. He made his own men watch as he cut strips of flesh from their bodies while they were still alive. Just hanging lumps of meat. Then Bobby cut their fingers off and put them in his pocket like they were pens. Rumour has it Bobby has all the fingers hanging in his office."

"Is that why they call him Bones?" asked Jackson.

"No, mate. They call him bones because he cut the leg off the first man, and beat the second guy to death with his femur." Harvey paused. "The fingers are just his trademark. The man is a bastard."

"And you're going to go and have a pint with him?" asked Reg.

Harvey didn't reply.

# OUT WITH A BANG

"CAN THEY SEW THEM BACK ON?" SAID THE RICH, articulate, grumble over the phone's speaker.

"They can, boss, but his hearing will be badly affected," said Tony.

"At least he wouldn't look like a freak. Has he told you who did it yet?"

"No, boss. He's been in surgery all morning having his ears removed from his hands."

"For god's sake. Who found him? Have we got that covered?"

"That's the most astonishing part, boss," said Tony, "he drove himself to hospital."

"With his ears screwed to his hands?" came the reply. "How did he steer?"

"I have no idea. But I checked the Jag, it's pretty beat up, and Les is still missing, so is the gear. I sent Jake over to the field to see if Les is around."

"And the other hospitals?"

"Nothing," said Tony.

"Well, I'm pretty sure I know who it was. But before we make a move, I need to be sure. He'll survive right?"

"Jay? Yeah, he'll just be uglier and a bit mutton."

"Tony?"

"Boss?"

"Go see his missus, will you? Sort her out, keep her sweet."

"Yeah, she's on her way here now," replied Tony.

"Couple of grand should do it."

"I'll sort it, boss."

Tony disconnected the call and walked back to the ward where Jay was. He caught hold of a nurse's arm.

"Excuse me, miss." The large African lady looked down at his hand on her arm. Tony removed it. "Sorry, can I ask you something?"

"How can I help?"

"My friend here, Jay Carter," he began.

"Oh, him." The lady gave Tony a look of contempt. "What do you need?"

"I'm worried whoever did this to him might come back and have another go, know what I mean?"

"No, I don't know what you mean."

"Well, the blokes that did it were pretty nasty. I reckon they'll be back to finish the job. Can we get him a private room?"

"You think this is a hotel, sir?" began the nurse. "We have very limited resources here, and I'm sure some patients have much more-"

"How much?"

"Excuse me?" she hissed.

"How much do you want? In your skyrocket, here you are, here's a grand, straight in your bin." Tony winked and slipped the bundle of twenties in her apron pocket. "Mum is the word, eh? When can we move him?"

The nurse held his gaze. She put her fingers into her pocket, pulled out the folded wad of cash and pinned it to Tony's chest with a long, brown finger. "You cannot *buy* a room here. Your friend is *not* in any danger and he, like the other patients we have, will be treated in an equal manner."

"Nothing we can do then?"

"Nothing you can do," the nurse said staccato.

"How about a drink? What time do you knock off, Gladys?" said Tony, reading her name badge.

"Visiting time is over. Say goodbye to your friend."

She turned and left Tony standing in the ward beside an old man's bed. The old man sat up with the covers over his legs and a newspaper laid across his lap. He looked up at Tony and smiled. "Hard to get that one," he said. "Gives a mean bed bath though." The old man winked at Tony, who chuckled and tapped the end of the bed thoughtfully.

"Good luck to you, mate," said Tony. He walked back to Jay's bed, slipping the curtain closed behind him.

"Jay," he called. Jay didn't respond. "Jay?" Tony gave his friend a nudge in his leg. Jay's eyes opened, but he was still under the effects of the painkillers. "Jay, I've got to go," began Tony. "Time's up, mate."

"Eh?" shouted Jay. "You what?"

"Shhh," said Tony with his finger on his lips. He acted out what he was saying while he repeated himself. "I," he said, pointing at himself, "have to go." He made his fingers walk then gestured to the door.

"You going?" shouted Jay.

"Shut up," said Tony. He stood and checked behind the curtain to make sure a nurse wasn't around, then pulled a Glock handgun from his waistband and held his finger up to his lips again. Then he gave Jay a mobile phone. It was a cheap Nokia burner with one number on speed dial, Tony's number. "Anything you need, just call." He gave Jay a serious nod, then stood and pulled the curtain back just as Carli, Jay's wife, was walking through the ward.

"How is he?" she asked with concern on her face.

Tony pulled the curtain closed behind him and stood in the ward with Carli. "Listen," he began, "it's pretty nasty. But don't worry, we're dealing with it."

"Don't worry?" Carli cried. "He had his-"

"Carli, easy, hear me out." Tony held his hands up, and then pulled another wad of cash from his pocket. "He'll be off work for a few weeks. Take this, it's from the boss, and if you need more, just call me, okay?"

"I don't want your money, Tony."

"It's not my money, it's the boss'. Just take it. It'll keep you ticking over."

Carli snatched the money from Tony's hand and brushed past him. Tony made his exit before Jay began shouting again.

He stepped out into the car park, lit a cigarette, and stood looking at all the cars. No sign of company. Two uniformed policemen headed towards the hospital's main entrance. They walked past Tony.

"Evening gentlemen," he said to them.

"Evening," one of them responded.

Tony pulled his phone from his pocket and hit redial. "Alright, boss, it's me, I reckon we ought to put a couple of blokes on the hospital."

"Do you think that's necessary?"

"If they come back for him, he won't stand a chance."

"If they meant for him to die, they would have killed him."

"So what was the point in cutting his ears off then?"

"That, Tony, was a message from them to me."

"Are we sending a reply?"

"They found Les, Tone."

"What's the news, boss?" asked Tony.

"Old bill found him this morning." There was a pause. "Stabbed in the eye with his own knife."

"Jesus, boss," said Tony with a grimace.

"Yeah, well, we aren't going to sit on our arses crying, Tone. We're going to make a plan. Meet me in the Spread Eagle tomorrow lunchtime."

"You want me to go see Julie?"

"I went to see Julie myself. Les was an old mate. But thanks, Tone, yeah. Get some rest."

Tony strolled across to his Ford in the far corner of the car park. He liked to park it away from the other cars so it stood out, and he could see if anyone was waiting in the cars nearby. He hit the button on the key fob, and the indicators flashed in the dim, early evening light.

Tony flicked his cigarette butt and watched the glowing lit tip spin through the air then extinguish on the wet tarmac. He opened the door of the car, climbed in and pulled it closed behind him. So much had happened, and he knew things were going to get a lot worse before they got better. If he was right, and it was the Albanians that had pulled the stunt, then things were going to get very messy. He sighed and laid his head back on the headrest for a moment before putting the keys in the ignition, and triggering the detonator on the explosive device connected to the ignition coil.

# 4

## EARLY DAYS

HARVEY SWIRLED THE REMAINS OF HIS PINT AT THE BOTTOM of his glass. It was one of the things he was dreading about going undercover. Not the danger, he could handle himself. Not the risk of death, he was ready for that provided it was quick, and he took the bloke with him. It was drinking alcohol; he hated the feeling of not being in control. But he would deter the people he was aiming to cosy up to if he didn't drink. It would raise a few eyebrows. So Harvey sucked it up and ordered another pint.

He was sitting at the bar of the Pied Piper on the edge of Canning Town. An old bloke sat on the end of the bar. A group of underage or barely legal kids sat in a booth in the corner. Three blokes about Harvey's age stood at the bar six feet away. It wasn't a particularly nice pub or even a big pub. But it had a bar, and that was all the clientele required. The types of people that drank in there did not require mirrors, marble or make-up. The men drank beer or spirits, and the women drank wine. Anything out of the ordinary would draw unnecessary attention, and the Pied Piper was not a pub where you wanted to be noticed.

EARLY DAYS • 25

Harvey ordered his second pint and waited patiently. He was playing the part of a bloke whose girlfriend lived nearby. If he was asked, he'd complain that she was driving him crazy and he needed to get out for a pint. The guy behind the bar turned the TV on. It was a decent sized flat screen mounted to the corner of the room so it could be seen from anywhere in the pub. Harvey wasn't into football, but he watched the game anyway. The red team were winning, the blue team weren't. *Good match*, he thought.

Harvey remembered the eighties when the football riots had escalated. West Ham fans would chase Chelsea fans along Green Street. Policemen and horses would line the road outside the Boleyn. It had been enough to put Harvey off the sport for life. He watched the players roll around with barely a scrape and felt ashamed that they were grown men. It was like watching kids play.

One of the men beside Harvey cheered when the red team missed an opportunity. "What, you supporting Chelsea now, Doug?"

"No, Trev, but if United win then West Ham will be relegated, but if Chelsea win, we'll stay in, just."

"I often wonder if it wouldn't be better to just go down a league. At least then we'd win a few games next season," said the one called Trev.

Harvey didn't look at the men, he just watched the match.

"Who you going for?"

Harvey heard the man's question but ignored him.

"Oy, dopey, who you going for?" said Trev.

Harvey turned his head to look at the man.

"What, are you special or something, mate? I asked you a question."

Harvey didn't reply.

"Jesus, we got a live one here, boys," said Trev, putting his pint down on the bar.

"The blue team," said Harvey without looking away.

"Oh, it talks, does it?" said Trev, looking to his two friends to see if they were laughing. "The blue team, eh?"

"Leave off, Trev," said Doug. "The bloke is just having a quiet pint. He don't want you in his face."

"Well, looks like you're losing, pal," said Trev.

Harvey didn't reply. He turned back to the TV, lifted his glass and eyed the men as he took a large mouthful of the rancid beer.

The door opened, and two big men stepped in out the cold. They wore old, scruffy, leather jackets, faded jeans and trainers. Harvey watched them in the reflections of the window as they stood at the bar on the other side of Harvey.

One of the newcomers ordered two Stellas in an Eastern European accent.

"Cheeky bastard," said Trev quietly to his two mates. "Who the bloody hell do they think they are?"

"They're just having a beer, Trev, calm down. What's the matter with you tonight?"

"What's the matter with me?" ranted Trev. "Did you hear him order the beer? Bloody Albanians. These lot burned down the boozer last night and then come strolling in here for a swift half. I want to ram it down their throats, Doug."

"Calm down, it probably weren't *them*."

"How do you know that?" said Trev. "How do you know these pricks haven't come in here to size the place up so they can burn it down later?"

"I *don't* know that, Trev," said Doug. "But it's the boss' place, and we'd do well not to smash it up and get the mob down here. The boss wants this place intact. He said he's got a plan for the Albies."

"Shouldn't let them in," said Trev.

"Another pint please, mate," said Harvey. He nodded to the barman.

"Same again?"

"Yeah, mate. Please."

"Ain't seen you around here before."

"That's because I've never been in here before," said Harvey.

"What's the occasion?" asked the barman.

"What are you, a copper?" said Harvey.

"No, mate, just making conversation," said the barman. "Take it easy, eh?"

"Yeah, sorry, mate," said Harvey, going into full undercover mode. "The bird is upstairs in the flat with the hump about something. I had too much to drink to drive home, so I came over here to get away from her. Is that allowed?"

"Yeah, mate, of course. We've all been there. Ain't that right, boys?" The barman gestured to the three men watching the match.

"Yeah," said Doug, disinterested, "join the club."

"Where are you from?" asked the barman.

"You ask a lot of questions."

"Just being friendly, pal," said the barman. He held out his hand. "I'm Lee," he said.

Harvey shook Lee's hand but said nothing.

"I didn't get your name, mate."

"No, you didn't, did you?" said Harvey. "Best we keep it that way."

"Suit yourself," said the barman.

Harvey raised his glass to his mouth just as the man beside him accidentally bumped his arm. Harvey spilt beer down his t-shirt. He froze and stared ahead of him over the bar. He felt the eyes of the Albanian bore into him. Testing him.

Doug, Trev and their mate all fell silent.

"Barman," said Harvey, "fat bloke here owes me a pint."

"I understand English," said the big man in a thick Eastern European accent.

"Good for you. So where's my pint?"

"Maybe you should learn how to hold your beer. Barman, get him half, maybe he will find it easier to hold." The man slapped a twenty-pound note on the bar. "Keep the change."

"Boys, boys, boys, no trouble in here tonight, please," said the barman. "Take your argument outside. Trevor, do the honours, will you?"

"Gladly," said Trev, putting his beer on the bar. He walked towards the door and held it open. A cold breeze blew in, and Harvey saw in the mirror behind the bar that it had started raining outside. "Right, tweedle-dee and tweedle-dumber, out."

Neither of the Albanian men moved.

Harvey remained motionless.

"Did you hear me?" said Trev. "We don't want your kind in here. Out." Trev stared the pair up and down and took a step towards them. They immediately dropped their glasses and turned to face Trev.

The man closest to Harvey pulled his massive arm back to throw a punch. Harvey watched in the mirror, then raised his own left arm. He hooked it into the crook of the man's arm and stamped down on the back of his knee. The Albanian buckled as Harvey dragged his weight back, smashing the back of his head on the hard wooden bar. He crumpled to the floor out cold.

The other man stood shocked, then squared up to face Harvey and Trev, expecting a blow from either man.

"You speak English?" asked Harvey calmly.

The man nodded. He knew he was outnumbered.

"Take your mate, and go," said Harvey. "Don't come back."

Trev held the door open again, and the big man dragged his friend into the rain.

"Nicely done, mate," said Trev. "What's your name?"

Harvey considered ignoring the question. He stared at the man who ten minutes before had been picking a fight with him. It had all been part of the plan. "Gerry."

"Nice to meet you, Gerry," said Trev, shaking Harvey's hand. "This is Doug and the quiet one there is Sid."

Harvey nodded at them in greeting.

"I'm surprised you didn't just lump them when he spilt your pint."

"Waiting for the moment, weren't I?" said Harvey. "I can't stand Albanians."

"You waited long enough," said Trev. "I thought it was going to kick off. How do you know they were Albanian?"

"BO and cheap leather jackets," replied Harvey.

"Fair enough. Can I get you a beer, Gerry?"

"Tell you what," said Harvey, "why don't we let tweedle-dee and tweedle-dumber get a round?" Harvey held up the twenty pounds the big Albanian had left behind and gave a half grin.

---

Melody woke the next morning with a message on her phone from Harvey telling her that the Albanians had made contact and he'd sent a message back to them. He expected things to heat up any day, but he would stay away from headquarters until it's over.

She rolled out of bed and stretched. She looked back at her girlfriend who was still sleeping, then dressed in yoga pants and a hooded sweater to go for a run. She ran along the river and into the old docks. There were no cars to avoid, and the relative peace meant she could let her head mull over the case.

She felt slightly helpless. Harvey was in the thick of it as usual, but it would be impossible for Melody and Reg to have his back if he was holed up in some pub. They relied on effective comms from Harvey but so far, all they had was the SMS he'd sent her that morning.

What did that mean? What message had he sent to the Albanians?

Before Harvey had left headquarters, Frank had insisted on Melody inserting a chip under the skin on his neck, so they could always trace his whereabouts. He'd spent most of the night in the Pied Piper, and knowing that Harvey didn't drink, Melody guessed that he would have been steaming drunk by the time he'd left.

Harvey had taken a tumble off Tower Bridge six months previously wearing an explosive vest. He'd taken down known-terrorist Al Sayan, but the explosion and the thought of him dying had rocked Melody. She had cried more than she ever thought she would. It was then that she realised she had feelings for Harvey. It was hard not to. He was a good man at heart; his moral compass was tuned. He was also a man's man, as tough as they come. He was desirable in every way, except for his very obscured past. She'd been with Frank when they had found the boiled remains of Sergio, Harvey's sister's rapist, and she'd seen Harvey at work. He was ruthless, yet he was gentle when he'd pulled Melody's half-drowned body from the ocean. He was cold-hearted and unforgiving, yet warm when Denver, the team's old driver, had been killed. He'd held her. Now Harvey was putting himself in danger yet again, and it didn't seem to phase him. Perhaps he'd never had someone to care for him. Maybe if he knew she cared, he'd stop and think. But if Harvey knew how she felt, the whole team dynamic would be changed, and she might lose him forever.

She ran on, pushing herself hard through the biting cold. The best she could do was to be there for him when he needed. She could watch Harvey's little icon on Reg's tracking screen as often as she could to keep tabs on him, and make sure she was never too far away to help if he needed it.

She showered, dressed in her cargo pants, boots and tank top beneath a clean hooded sweater, and left her girlfriend asleep. It was still only five am. Melody drove a little two-seater Mazda convertible. The roof stayed up most the year.

Her phone rang as she pulled out of her apartment and she snatched it from her pocket in case it was Harvey. It was Frank.

"Sir?"

"Mills, good morning," said Frank.

"What's the plan?" asked Melody.

"Have you heard from Stone?"

"Yeah, he says he'll stay away until this blows over, doesn't want to blow his cover."

"Okay. Next time you talk to him, tell him I want a daily debrief, not via you."

"Yes, sir, I'll tell him."

"Good. I want you to get down to Romford. Queens Hospital," said Frank.

"What's there?"

"Car bomb, known suspect. Remember the ears?"

"How could I forget?"

"Well, this guy was visiting him. He left the hospital got into his car and well..."

"Okay, sir. What are your thoughts?"

"My thoughts, Mills? I think this is getting out of hand and we're closing the proverbial barn door."

"My sentiments exactly. It's going to take some mopping up, sir."

"I agree. Sadly we have Stone in the thick of it, and he's not likely to be diligently mopping anything up. Whatever it is he's doing, you can be sure he'll be making a mess."

Four big men banged their pint glasses on the bar of the Pied Piper. It was a lock-in, and the doors had been locked five hours ago. They cheered loudly, and fistfuls of money exchanged hands. Harvey connected his sweaty hand with his opponent's, and they began to arm wrestle.

Harvey's fist gripped Doug's. Each man tried hard to get his fingers on top. Their hands were sweaty and slick, their shoulders and arms ached from the previous rounds, and Harvey, the undisputed champion, stared into the eyes of his opponent. His face remained impassive, his mouth unsmiling. He pushed hard; each inch of progress was locked off with Harvey's tired bicep. Move an inch, lock it off, repeat. Doug strained and squirmed, his feet fought for grip as he tried in vain to find purchase and a new advantage. Harvey took a deep breath, released it slowly through his gritted teeth, then slammed Doug's hand onto the bar.

There was a loud uproar, money exchanged hands again, Trev hooted loudly, and the three other spectators sank their drinks.

"No more," said Harvey. "Home time." He feigned a little drunken balance issue and looked at each of the men with one of his eyes closed.

"You think she's still mad at you?" asked Trev.

"Who?" asked Harvey, then he remembered the lie he'd told about his girlfriend being upset about something. It was the reason for him being in the pub in the first place. "Whatever. Catch you around boys."

"See ya later, Gerry," called Trev.

Harvey walked in the direction of some council flats. He took turns down a rabbit warren of alleyways and roads to make sure he wasn't being followed, and then found a small cab firm on the main road to Canning Town. He sat in the back of the car and directed the driver to the row of shops a hundred yards from his home, where he stripped, showered and fell into bed.

He wasn't drunk. He'd managed to stay sober by drinking as much water as he could from the tap in the Pied Piper's bathroom. Each time he finished a beer, he'd excuse himself and drink more water than he had beer. He was happy that he'd made a good impression. Taking the Albanian down had been a decent way to infiltrate the firm, and then the drinking time had helped. Usually getting into a firm would take months, but Harvey didn't have months. The quicker he could get through this undercover piece, the sooner he could get back to normal, whatever that was.

He fell asleep wondering what exactly normal meant to him. Harvey's life had been far from normal before he'd been brought into the team. But ever since, they'd stopped a ring of sex traffickers, prevented a terrorist attack on St Paul's and saved a priceless jade buddha from being stolen. During which, he'd been shot at and blown up, drowned, and now, he even had a dog. How did any of that happen?

He woke with a start and saw the bright light through his windows. It took a few moments for him to remember what had happened, and why he'd slept so late. It was early afternoon. There were missed calls and messages from Melody on his phone. He dialled her number. The number was stored, but for Harvey, it was easier to dial from memory than it was to go through his contacts list.

"Harvey, what's going on?"

"You tell me. I just woke up."

"You sound sleepy. You do realise what time it is, don't you?"

"Yeah, it was a late one, made some good progress with the firm."

"New besties?"

"You're my bestie, Melody. Where are you?"

"I'm at Queens Hospital in Romford. Remember the guy with the ears?"

"Yeah."

"Well, he had a visitor, one of his firm, a guy called Tony. Someone planted a bomb in his car while he was visiting."

"Tony?" said Harvey. "Not Tony Hunt?"

"Yeah, that's him, or was him," Melody corrected herself. "Did you know him?"

"I knew *of* him. He was one of Thomson's blokes back in the day. What was the name of the bloke with the ears?"

"Jay Robins," replied Melody.

"And the guy with the eye?" asked Harvey.

"Les."

"Les Fitzpatrick?" asked Harvey.

"Yeah, that rings a bell, I think so."

"It's weird, the boys I met last night haven't said a word about anyone called Tony, Les, or Jay, and the only talk of Albanians were the two that walked into the pub. I would have thought that a car bombing in the firm would have got around like wildfire. Maybe Bobby is keeping the news on the down low. But it *does* sound like the remnants of Thomson's old mob. Maybe Bobby Bones moved in when I took Thomson down a couple of years ago. Where's their manor?"

"All over. Stratford, East Ham, Bow. There's a few bars and pubs, most of the bookies. Anything cash with heavy foot traffic and they're involved by the looks of things."

"Bobby had a keen eye for an opportunity," said Harvey. "Most of those blokes were loyal to the letter. Thomson had been running Stratford for years, but not East Ham, that used to be John's."

"Your old man?"

"My foster father."

"So Bobby cleaned up," said Melody. "He did well."

"Yeah, but has he got the clout to keep these Albanians out? I doubt it. Most of these younger lot coming up are sloppy and into drugs. The Albanians are professionals, born into the life."

"We need to meet," said Melody. "We'll need a plan to put a stop to all this. We'll have to do something soon, the media are all over it. There's a crew here now. They love it; it's like Christmas for them."

"Stay away from the cameras, Melody. The last thing I need is for you to be recognised."

"What are you saying? What does that matter?"

"Well, I might need an angry girlfriend to get me out of the pub."

"Oh, right. What have you told them?"

"My girlfriend is a psycho. That's my excuse for staying in the pub."

"Right. So I may need to storm in and walk you out by the ear?"

Harvey laughed. "No, Gerry wouldn't stand for that. But I might need a bird, if you know what I mean."

"Class, Harvey," said Melody. "Who's Gerry?"

"He makes a special appearance every now and then, gets drunk with the guys, smashes them at arm wrestling and shows them how to deal with a pair of Albanian troublemakers."

"I'm not sure I could date a guy called Gerry," said Melody.

Harvey heard the smirk on Melody's face. "Yeah, well, I'm not sure I could date a psycho bird who drives me to drink."

"Touché."

"How's Frank?"

"Mad that you're not debriefing him."

"Good."

"What do you mean good?" said Melody. "Please call him after this call. He just moans at me when you don't give him a debrief."

Harvey laughed again. "Yeah that Gerry is a right bastard."

"Keep me posted," said Melody.

Harvey disconnected the call.

# 5

# THE BEAST WITHIN

IT WAS EARLY EVENING WHEN HARVEY STEPPED BACK INTO the Pied Piper. The pub was busier. The same old man stood at the end of the bar, the same kids sat in the booth, but there were a few additions. The TV was off, and the jukebox was on, loudly playing the type of music that Harvey heard, but wouldn't remember two minutes later. Two women and two men stood at the bar laughing and joking. It clearly wasn't their first or last glass of wine that night.

At the end of the bar stood Doug, Trev, Sid, and the three other men who had joined them for the lock-in the previous night.

"He's back for more. What d'ya say there, Gerry, can I get you a pint, mate?" said Trev.

"Yeah sure. Thanks, Trev," replied Harvey.

"We were just talking about those two Albanians. Sid reckons they'll be back with their mates. What do you think, Gerry?"

"Wasn't it Albanians that burnt down the pub up the road?" asked Harvey.

"Yeah, we think so," said Doug. "How do you know about that?"

"Just some bloke at work, lives nearby and doesn't shut up, likes the sound of his own voice, know what I mean?"

"Yeah, well, best to keep that kind of info under your hat, Gerry. That was the boss' favourite pub, and he's not happy about it. They've burned down two of his pubs and three of his bookies in the past two weeks."

Harvey acted surprised. "What the hell? Why? I mean, if can ask, I don't want to overstep."

"It's okay, Gerry. Keep it to yourself though, will you? It's going to kick off. The boss don't take this kind of stuff laying down."

"Yeah, no worries. We should get a bunch of blokes together and torch the bastards one by one."

Doug chuckled. "Well, that's not too far from the plan. Anyway, cheers." Doug raised his glass and Harvey chinked his own against the side of it.

Trev came back into the pub holding his phone. He walked directly to Doug. "Boss just called. He's on his way and said we need to clear this place. He's arranged something."

"Clear the pub?" said Doug. "What for? Any idea?"

"No, mate. Get Lee to turn the jukebox off, and I'll get everyone out."

Doug leaned across the bar. "Lee?"

Lee looked along the bar. "What's up? I'm serving."

"Well stop serving and kill the music," said Doug.

The music was cut shortly after, and Trev shouted over the moans and complaints. "Listen, I've been asked to clear the pub. So drink up, you all need to be gone in five minutes."

More complaints, tuts and dirty looks were aimed at Trev as he rejoined the group of men.

"You always have that effect on people, Trev?" asked Harvey, falling further into the character of Gerry.

Trev chuckled. "Yeah, although at least this time I didn't get a pint glass lobbed at me." He turned back to the crowd. "Four minutes, people."

Harvey began to finish his pint. "Have I got time for a quick shot? I'll neck it and be gone."

"Mate, relax, you can stay. You're with us. Get a pint, get me one too while you're at it," said Doug.

Harvey raised two fingers at Lee the barman in a peace sign. People began to filter out, and soon only the men were left in the quiet bar.

"They really listened to you this time, Trev. Amazing," said Sid.

Doug leaned towards Harvey. "Last time he did it a couple of geezers refused to budge, so Trev had to get all Jackie Chang on them."

"I didn't get Jackie Chang on no-one, Doug. It was more Chuck Norris." Trev performed a poor impression of Chuck Norris preparing to fight.

"Oy," said Sid. He raised his finger at Trev and looked him square in the eye. "One does not impersonate Chuck Norris. The man is a legend."

Trev laughed. "Yeah, apparently, when Chuck Norris goes to Rome, they do what he does."

"Apparently Chuck Norris can lick both his elbows at the same time," said one of the men.

"I heard Chuck Norris doesn't cheat death, he wins fair and square," said Doug.

The group were in high spirits considering the boss was coming, who Harvey presumed to be Bobby 'Bones' Carnell. True to Harvey's thoughts, the laughter stopped when the lights of three cars pulled into the pub car park and shone through the opaque glass in the door.

Doug leaned into Harvey again. "Do yourself a favour and just keep quiet. He's a nice guy, but he won't like hearing from you before an introduction."

"Yeah, no worries. I can leave if you want," said Harvey.

"No mate, stay, drink." Doug smiled and winked.

The doors of the pub opened and two men stepped inside, nodded to the group of men and held the door for Bobby Carnell to enter the room. He looked the typical East End gangster with a long Kashmir coat, thick horn-rim glasses and immaculate shoes. He walked to the bar where a scotch and soda waited for him. The two men that accompanied him stood beside him talking. Harvey noticed the word bones spelt out on the back of his hand in faded tattoo ink.

More cars pulled into the car park, and more men entered the pub, who Doug seemed to know. He nodded at them. Then the man beside Bobby Bones caught Doug's attention and gestured to the doors. Doug tapped Trev with his foot. "Go and bolt the doors will you, Trev."

Trev nodded and disappeared into the throng.

"Quiet," somebody called. The room fell silent, and all eyes fell on Bobby 'Bones' Carnell.

"Thanks everyone for coming," began Bobby. "I know you're all busy. I know Christmas is coming, and most of you have families to look after, so I'll be straight to the point." He sipped at his scotch. "In case some of you don't know my story, when I was a little boy, three bigger boys tried to bully me." He left a pause for the image to take hold in the minds of his men. "I waited patiently." Bobby's voice was gravelly, rough and very cockney. "Until one day, a few weeks later, I found one of them boys on his own. I gave the kid a hiding, and then some, and then I cut his finger off and stamped on his head one last time for good measure. Over the following months, I caught up with all three of them kids. They all got the same treatment, no favours, no matter how hard the last one pleaded. They all got the same hiding. And they all lost a finger. I've still got them in a jar as a reminder never to let anyone fuck me over." He took another sip of his drink and put the glass down. There was a fresh one waiting for him.

"Right now, gentlemen, I see the need to remind a few people not to fuck me over again, and I'll be honest, I need your help to do it." He stared around at all the men. His eyes settled on Harvey's for longer than necessary. Harvey stared back. Bobby moved on.

"There is outside two vans and all the tools we need. We're leaving in two minutes. Drink up. We'll be back for supper."

---

"Tenant, where's Stone?" asked Frank as he walked down the headquarter's mezzanine stairs from his office. He stopped at Reg's command centre, which comprised of twelve twenty-four inch screens mounted on the wall in three rows of four, and a super-computer Reg had named LUCY. It monitored the whereabouts of any GPS enabled device, which was typically phones that belonged to suspects, victims and the team, and tracking chips, one of which was inserted under Harvey's skin. There were more in his phone, in his watch, in his jacket, and on his motorbike.

"He left the Pied Piper five minutes ago, sir. I'm watching him now." Reg pointed up at the left-hand screen in the centre row. He's not using his bike though, so I can only assume he's with a target."

"Mills," called Frank across the headquarter's open space.

"Sir?"

"Has Stone contacted you in the past hour?"

"Negative, sir. I sent him a message but no response as yet."

"You told him to call in as I asked?"

"Yes, sir. He said he would."

"Get yourself ready," said Frank. "Jackson?"

"Sir?" Jackson was laying under the team's VW Transporter van, which served as a mobile operations unit. "Get cleaned up, you're heading out. Tenant, you too."

"Remember," called Frank over the noise of Jackson's tools being wiped and put away and Melody's cabinets being slammed shut, "we're observing only. We're not taking anyone down. But we are keeping an eye on our own. If Stone doesn't want to report in, we'll have to find our own information."

Melody dropped three large peli-cases into the back of the van. One contained Steiner binoculars and a sighting scope. One contained night-vision goggles, and the other contained her prized Diemaco rifle. The Diemaco was Melody's favourite of the rifles they kept in the armoury and was her go-to weapon for long distance.

Reg fired up the two computers in the back of the van and took his place at his bench, which ran the full length of the van's cargo area. Two screens sat atop the bench, and the rear windows were fully blacked out.

"We set?" asked Melody.

"Good to go," confirmed Reg.

Jackson fired up the engine and closed the driver's door. The computers in the back of the van gave Reg access over SSL VPN to LUCY, which meant he could control the head-quarter's doors, as well as the telephones, heating, and lighting. He hit the shortcut for the doors, and the motor above the concertina shutter jumped into life. The doors dragged across and Jackson reversed out.

"Where we heading, Reg?" asked Jackson.

"They're at Old Street now. You know the way?"

"Yeah, lived here all my life, Reg. Just keep me posted if their position changes."

"Where exactly are you from, Jackson?" asked Melody.

"Me? I moved around a bit. Grew up in Essex, moved to East London, then out to Kent when my old man died. Landed a job at the local track and started driving."

"So how did you wind up on the force?"

"My old man was a copper. Mum always pushed me towards it, but I wanted to drive. So I guess it's a bit of both. Decent pension and I would say the hours are great but anything deeper than the Met, and the hours are messed up. I did a bit for SO10, crazy hours. That's where I met Frank, and Denver too actually. He was a nice guy."

"You knew Denver?" asked Reg.

"Yeah, worked with him a few times on a few busts. Top bloke."

"Yeah, he was," said Melody.

"One thing I can't seem to work out though," said Jackson, "who do we work for? It's not SO10 as far as I can tell, and it's obviously not SO19."

"We're unofficial. We're supposed to get status soon, but for the time being, all credit goes to SO10. We're an unofficial arm."

"Expendable?"

"Yeah, in short. As long as we keep performing, we'll be made official. But it's slow going."

"Stone has joined the A1 towards Highbury," said Reg from behind.

"Highbury? Jesus. What's he mixed up in?"

"What's our ETA?"

"I'd say we're twenty-five minutes out," said Jackson. "What's he like?"

"Who? Harvey?"

"Yeah, bit wild from what I gather."

"Wild?" said Reg. "He's the nicest lunatic I know."

"Lunatic?"

"No, he's not," said Melody. "He's a nice guy. He just had a different upbringing, and has a particular skill set that compliments the rest of us."

"So, he's the one with dirty hands then?"

"You could put it like that."

"Is it me, or has he just got this stare going on? Like you ask him a question, he doesn't reply, but he doesn't need to. It's crazy."

"Powerful, isn't it?" said Melody.

"What about Frank?"

"Best boss I've had," said Melody.

"Yeah, he's okay, he's fair. He's good at letting us do what we need to do. I like that," said Reg. "Okay, friendly chat is over. Harvey has stopped in a side street in Highbury. He's moving towards what looks to be a pub. Is this whole case going to revolve around pubs?"

"Whereabouts?" asked Jackson.

"Off Highbury Road, the Jumping Jack."

Jackson put his foot down and overtook the car in front. "ETA, ten minutes."

Melody checked her Sig and unboxed the binos. "Reg, find us somewhere to hole up. I've got an idea he isn't visiting old friends, and I need to get the suspects on camera." She held on as Jackson slid the van around a long corner.

"I've got it, there's a supermarket opposite. We can park up in the car park and get a decent view," said Reg. "What do you think is going to happen, Melody?"

"Well, he's with some pretty bad men, who just had their pub burned down, so I'd say it's not a housewarming party."

---

Fifteen men sat quietly in the two vans outside the Jumping Jack, each of them armed with a mixture of bats, short poles, machetes and knives. Harvey was in the first van. Nobody spoke. Each man was psyching himself up for what was about to happen. The man in the passenger seat, who had been stood next to Bobby Bones in the pub, turned in his seat and spoke quietly but firmly. "Trev, Doug, go in and make sure they're there. Order a pint and send me a text."

The remaining men waited a long two minutes before the text came through. He read the message aloud. "There's about thirty of them, but we'll catch them off guard. Turn right through the doors." The man looked around at the men sat in the back of the van. Most were staring at the floor or the ceiling, breathing hard, tensing up. Harvey stared back at the man, "In and out boys, the van is leaving in two minutes." He paused grinning. "Ready? Go, go, go."

The rear doors of the van opened, and the men filed out. Harvey stood fourth in line. The only two blokes he knew were already in there. Harvey had taken a bat from the pile of tools on the floor of the van. He carried his Sig and always had his knife on him. But he didn't want to stand out, so he chose the bat.

The first two men walked through the doors and held them open, leaving Harvey in number two position. He stepped through onto the typical worn, red pub carpet. His eyes hit the mirror above the bar, and he saw a group of big men behind the door to his right.

Harvey stepped around the door and swung at the first man. The table erupted as the Albanians stood up, and more of Bobby's firm appeared from behind Harvey in a chaos of swinging bats and blades. Harvey turned his attention to the far corner where more Albanians had risen and were making their way through the crowd, edging away from the fracas. A woman screamed and ran for the far doors, but a surge of large Albanian men forced her backwards.

Leaving the first fight, Harvey met the oncoming group

head on. He took the first down with a downward swing of the bat, then jabbed the second one with the butt of the handle. He heard a bottle being smashed and caught the movement in the corner of his eye; he ducked back, and the broken glass shot past his face. Harvey dropped down and shattered the man's knees. Another man kicked the bat from his hands, so Harvey instinctively drew his knife, stood up close to the man and drove the blade into his neck. A head-butt finished him off, and the man fell to the floor.

Harvey span and saw the doors opening; Bobby's men were leaving. The two minutes were up. But two more Albanians stood in Harvey's way. They were the last two remaining. Doug held the door open. "Gerry, go, now."

Harvey stepped forward, blocked a wild punch and drove his knife into the first guy's throat. He pulled it out with a sucking sound as the second man swung for Harvey's face. Harvey dodged back quickly then lunged forwards, sinking the blade into the man's chest. He walked past the dying man and ripped the knife out, letting the Albanian drop to the floor behind him.

Another wounded Albanian rolled around on the carpet beside the front door. His arm was broken, and his nose had burst across his face. Harvey picked up the man's foot and dragged him outside.

"Cheers, Doug," said Harvey as he stepped outside, letting the man's head bounce on the hard pavement. He dragged him to the van, ignoring his moans and outbursts in a language Harvey didn't understand.

Harvey saw the familiar shape of a VW Transporter a hundred yards away in the car park of the supermarket. He could just make out the passenger door opening and a leg stepping down.

"Someone, give me a lift up with this, will you?"

"Who's that?" someone asked.

"I don't know, do I? I didn't stop to ask his name," said Harvey.

"We don't bloody want him in here."

"Yes, we do," said Dom from the passenger seat. "The boss will love that, nice work. Get him inside, and let's fuck off before the old bill turns up."

"Go, we're in," said Harvey once he'd pulled the doors closed. He sat with his feet on the Albanian's back and removed his knife from its sheave to clean it on a rag from the van floor.

"Holy shit, Gerry," said Doug. "Think we found us a new man, Dom."

The man in the passenger seat turned around. "Is that right?"

"Did you see that in there?" said Doug. "He stabbed some geezer in the throat, then without blinking turned and stabbed his mate in the chest." Doug whooped. "It was legendary."

"Did we lose anyone?" asked Harvey, ignoring the remarks.

"Yeah, two fellas down. They're in the back of the other van."

"Serious?"

"One had his face slashed, the other is unconscious," said Dom. "Why do you ask?"

"Just checking the odds. Thirty against fifteen, none of them are standing, and thirteen of us are. Plus, we got a prisoner." Harvey leaned into the corner of the van. "Pretty successful."

"Yeah, well, it'll be successful in a minute when the whole place goes up."

"What do you mean, Dom?" asked Doug.

"While we were in there doing the renovating, Charlie here made a few gas alterations. Didn't you, Charlie?" Dom turned to face the rear of the van and smiled in the darkness.

"I'd give it two minutes max. As soon as someone lights their next fag, it'll be game over," said Charlie. He was older than the rest of the men, smoked roll-ups and had a hard, weathered face.

Harvey hadn't known about the fire. He needed to text Melody in case she went inside, but couldn't risk it, being so close to the other guys in the van. He was shoulder to shoulder with the man next to him, who would easily see what Harvey was typing.

The van pulled to the side of the road and stopped. "Sit tight, lads," said the driver. "Let's wait for the fireworks."

The second van pulled up alongside the first, and all the men stared out the rear windows.

Nothing happened.

A car drove past the two vans heading towards the pub, and from the supermarket car park came the dark square shape of the VW. It stopped and waited for the car to pass, then moved on again. It had just passed the pub when the gas ignited.

---

"There he is," said Melody. "I know that swagger anywhere. What's he doing?" Melody opened the door and stepped down to get a clearer view.

"He's dragging someone behind him," said Reg.

"He's looking right at us," said Jackson. "He is a lunatic. If the Albanians come back out of that pub, he is toast."

"He's okay. Just hang back, give him some space and let him do his thing."

"They were only in there a couple of minutes. What do you think happened?" asked Jackson.

"Judging by the people that ran out, I'd say it kicked off pretty well, and by the looks of Harvey, the local firm came out on top," said Reg.

"That won't be the end of it. The Albanians won't take it lying down," said Melody. "Follow that second van, Jackson. If those injured locals are going to be in hospital for a while, it'd be a good place to catch up with them, get some answers. Let's go, Jackson, nice and slow."

Jackson pulled away, keeping the lights off until the vans were out of sight. They drove out the car park and onto the road beside the pub.

"Don't stop here, keep going," said Melody, just as the pub windows blew out, causing the van to rock to one side. "Go, go, go." Flames licked the roof of the van, shattered glass rained on the bodywork, and Reg's blacked-out windows lit up as they pulled out of the blast just in time.

Jackson floored the van and accelerated to the end of the road.

"What the hell was that?" said Reg.

"What way did they go?" asked Jackson.

"Harvey turned right according to LUCY."

They heard the sound of sirens in the distance. "Okay, let's ease up, get our bearings."

"I was not expecting that," said Jackson.

"You get to expect the unexpected when Harvey is involved," said Melody, grinning slightly.

"You find that funny?" said Jackson. "I swear my eyebrows singed through the glass."

Melody laughed. "Relax, they just answered our questions."

"What questions?"

"Are we onto the right firm and will there be a retaliation?"

"A retaliation? The Albanians won't take this lying down.

If there wasn't a war already, there is definitely one now."

"Good, we'll catch them faster," said Melody.

"And what if more people die?"

"Nobody wants that, Jackson."

"What about if Harvey is killed?"

"Don't talk like that."

"It's a possibility, Melody, not a wish."

"Harvey can take care of himself. Anyway, the question isn't about Harvey getting killed, it's about stopping innocent people dying as a result of the violence. Why the interest in Harvey?"

"There's no interest, Melody. I'm just being the caring team member."

"Well, how about we let Harvey do what he's good at, and we do our jobs and find him."

"Looks like they're heading back to East Ham," said Reg from the rear.

"Cheers, Reg," said Jackson. "Listen, Melody, I'm sorry. I shouldn't have overstepped the mark. I-"

"You didn't overstep the mark, Jackson. We're all a bit sensitive right now. We lost a good man a while back."

"Yeah, I get that. No hard feelings?"

"Whatever," said Melody. "Don't think too much on it."

"There's a great bagel shop near here, my treat."

"Ah," said Reg, "you've struck gold there, Jackson. Even Melody can't refuse a salt beef bagel."

Melody turned and smiled at Reg, then at Jackson. "Okay, but no more talk of-"

"Scout's honour," said Jackson, holding up his fingers in a scout salute.

"What about Harvey and his white van men?"

"Keep an eye on his location. We can't do much more than that. Besides," said Melody, "what's he going to do, torture the man? It's not the dark ages."

# 6

# THE BEAST'S TOUCH

THE ALBANIAN HUNG BY HIS BOUND WRISTS FROM A MEAT hook, swinging beside cow legs in the rear of Dave the Butcher's shop. He'd been stripped naked, and the break in his arms was visible against his skin; his body weight was pulling the break further apart, and the man's face was wrought with agony.

Dom, Doug and Harvey stood beside him.

"What a fat piece of crap," said Doug. "What're we going to do with him?"

Harvey was silent.

"We'll save him for the boss," said Dom. "He'll love this."

"Should I go, or what?" said Harvey.

"Go? Why go?" said Dom. "The boss will be over the bloody moon, mate. You just got yourself a job. No, Gerry, you're staying, mate."

A car door slammed a dull thud in the distance and footsteps approached. Harvey heard the door creak open but remained with his eyes on the Albanian.

"Well, well, well," said Bobby 'Bones' Carnell. "What do we have here?"

"He hasn't said anything yet, Bobby," said Dom. "We thought we'd let you have the first go on him."

"First go, eh?" said Bobby. "Whose idea was it to bring him back here?"

The three were silent, then Dom spoke up. "Gerry here dragged him out the pub. I brought him here. Was that wrong, Bobby?"

"Wrong? Why would that be wrong? What we have here is a little talking parrot, and boy, are we going to make him sing. Right, where are the tools?"

"What do you need, Bobby?" asked Doug.

"Pliers," said Bobby, "to start with. Actually, no, scrub that, Doug." Bobby turned to Harvey. "Gerry, isn't it?"

Harvey didn't reply. He just leaned on the wall with his arms folded.

"Dom tells me you're a bit of a hard nut."

"You should have seen him in there, Bobby," said Doug.

"Anyone can take a few men down, Doug. You just need big balls. Have you got big balls, Gerry?"

Harvey didn't reply.

"Tell you what, Gerry, why don't you get this fat waste of skin to tell us who and where his boss is?" He paused to look at Harvey's reaction. "Reckon you can do that? Let's see what you're made of."

Harvey pushed off the wall and walked towards the Albanian, whose eyes opened wide when he looked at Harvey's expression. Harvey stood in front of him. He blocked out Dom, Doug and Bobby Bones. It was just Harvey and the Albanian in the huge slaughterhouse.

"Do you have a name?" asked Harvey in a dull, flat tone.

The man eyed him. Beads of sweat had begun to form on his temple.

"One more time, and then I'll get to work," said Harvey. "Name."

Harvey walked behind the man. There were scars across his back, long, deep, and thick, like he'd been whipped a long time ago. His right calf featured the flat white scar of a deep burn. Harvey had seen scars like that before. It was the type of scar that gave a sense of empathetical pain just by looking at the twisted and melted flesh.

The man rattled off a long garbled sentence in Albanian, and then said, "Aleksander."

"Aleksander? You look like an Aleksander." Harvey turned to Dom. "Do we have any wood?"

"Wood? What do you want wood for?"

"An old pallet or something. Can I get some wood, please?"

Dom followed the chain of command and turned to Doug, who left the room.

"You understand English, Aleksander?"

Aleksander didn't reply.

Harvey completed his tour of the Albanian and returned to stand in front of him. "English, Aleksander?"

Aleksander nodded. His angry eyes had softened, giving a window of weakness for Harvey to reach into.

Harvey hated every minute of the charade. It wasn't the first time he'd tortured somebody. But in the past, his victims had deserved every second of the ordeal. Aleksander was just a villain, same as Dom and Doug. Harvey didn't care if Aleksander lived or died, or any of them. He didn't care if the man spoke or not, but he had to make the man talk. This was an opportunity for Gerry to impress Bobby Bones. Getting Aleksander to inform on his boss would ingratiate Gerry into the boss' good books and then maybe he could put a stop to everything, and get back to the team.

Harvey thought about how he missed his team. He'd never done that before.

"Are your family here, Aleksander? In London?"

Aleksander shook his head. "No."

"Are they in Albania?"

He nodded. "Yes, Albania, yes."

"And are you sending them money?"

He nodded again. "Yes, my mother and my sister."

"And your father?"

"He is dead," spat Aleksander. "He is traitor."

"So if you stop sending money home, what will happen to your mother and your sister?"

Aleksander didn't reply.

Doug came back into the room dragging two heavy wooden pallets. He let them fall to the floor.

"Can you break them up, please, Doug?" said Harvey. "I'm going to get a little campfire going to keep Aleksander warm."

Aleksander's eyes widened again.

"Do you like fire, Aleksander?"

Aleksander shivered with fear, and sweat began to run from his bald head down his unshaven face.

"You've been burned before, haven't you?" asked Harvey. "I saw the scar. Who did that?"

Aleksander didn't reply.

"Looks nasty." Harvey gauged the big man to be in his early forties. "Kosovo, right?"

Aleksander's eyes darted to Harvey's.

"I'm right, aren't I?"

"I saw the whip marks on your back too. You're a bad man, Aleksander, aren't you?"

"Fuck you."

Doug had smashed one of the pallets into firewood and stood back to watch the show. Bobby and Dom were enthralled by Harvey's calm composure, and the effect he was having on Aleksander.

"The thing is," began Harvey, as he bent down to pick up a few pieces of wood, "the Serbs weren't really organised enough, were they?" Harvey bent and began to arrange the wood. "I mean, they certainly weren't organised enough to capture one of the Albanian army and torture him unless, of course, you were a high ranking officer. But if you don't mind me saying, Aleksander, you haven't really got officer qualities, have you?"

"You know nothing," said Aleksander.

"No, those wounds on your back weren't done by the Serbs, were they?" said Harvey, ignoring the comment. Harvey had learned over the years that momentum, building up tension and leaning on sore points was the key to getting somebody to talk. Harvey hadn't been trained to evoke information from a captive, he'd taught himself. Some men broke easily and disappointed Harvey. It may have taken weeks for Harvey to practise his mantra of patience, planning and execution, only to eventually capture the sex offender he'd been targeting and have him confess within a few minutes. Harvey preferred the chase. He found that the longer the tension built up, the more information could be sought. The deeper the confession.

"The Serbs weren't known for that type of thing, Aleksander, they were fighting a war. But the Albanians? Well, you guys have always been partial to a bit of violence, right? But why would the Albanians do something like this to their own? Unless, of course, you were absconding?" Harvey looked Aleksander in the eye. "Is that it, Aleksander? Did you run away like a frightened little boy?" Harvey let the man absorb his words before he spoke again. "You were captured by your own, weren't you? Big men capturing a frightened little boy."

Harvey stepped to the side of the room where a large roll of tissue paper stood on its end beside a sink, presumably for the butcher to dry his hands after he'd washed them. He pulled off a long stream of paper and rolled it into a ball.

"They hurt you, didn't they?" asked Harvey. "They hurt you so badly, you hate them now." Harvey bent to stuff the paper beneath the pile of wood, which lay beneath Aleksander's feet.

"In fact, you've never been back, have you?" Harvey stood. "I don't think you've seen your mother or your sister in all this time." Harvey paused to read Alexander's pained expression. "I'm right, aren't I? They're trapped there because you ran away, and you're stuck here because you're a coward." Harvey found a box of matches on the tiled window ledge. He opened the box and stopped, poised to strike the match.

"Tell me, Aleksander, are you going to be a coward now, or are you going to face your fears?"

"I will tell you nothing," spat the Albanian.

"You're shaking, Aleksander," said Harvey slowly and coldly. "That's the fear. When did you last shake like this? Was it when you ran away from the battle? Or was it when you ran away from your captors?"

Harvey struck the match.

I long thin stream of urine came involuntarily from Aleksander.

"There it is," said Harvey. "No-one can stop the fear when it bites." Harvey held the match up in front of Aleksander. "There's just two things we need to know, and then all of this can stop, Aleksander."

"Aleksander's eyes were squinted, his lip had begun to tremble, and he hung his head as far back as he could.

"Who's your boss?" said Harvey. The match burned out, and he dropped it to the floor. "It's okay, we have a full box."

"Stop," said Aleksander. His voice had risen an octave, and the fear had shaken his rough tone.

"No, Aleksander, I will not stop."

Harvey struck another match.

"Who's your boss?"

"Ah," gasped Aleksander.

"Don't cry, little boy. I know you're frightened, but tell me, and then all of this will be over."

"No."

"Aleksander, I won't waste this match."

"Luan."

"Ah, Luan. There we go." Harvey blew on the match, and the flame extinguished, leaving only smoke. Harvey dropped the match to the floor and pulled a fresh one out.

"Last name, Aleksander." Harvey sat the tip of the match on the paper.

Aleksander's head rolled forward, and tears fell from his fat face.

"Are those tears of shame, Aleksander?" asked Harvey. "No need for shame, you're just following your path and your daddy's path. He was a traitor too, wasn't he?"

Harvey lit the third match.

"Last name. Last chance."

Aleksander didn't reply.

Harvey waved the flame under Aleksander's face. The man's head sat bolt upright.

"I said, last name?"

"Duri," said Aleksander quietly, and dejected.

Harvey puffed the match out and dropped it to the tiled floor. He pulled another one from the box and sat the tip on the striking paper again.

"Okay, last question," said Harvey. "Where do we find him?"

Aleksander didn't respond.

"So now you have two options, Aleksander. Option one." Harvey made sure he caught Aleksander's eye. "You tell me where I can find him, and you die a quick, clean death. There's honour in there, somewhere."

Aleksander didn't respond.

"Option two, and I don't like this one myself, Aleksander, but if you don't tell me where I can find him, I'll burn you alive." Harvey held his finger up. "And not only will I burn *you* alive, but I'll carry on looking, and when I do find Luan Duri, I'll make sure he knows that you informed, and I'll make sure your mother and your sister are punished back in whatever mud hole they live in."

Harvey moved closer and whispered to Aleksander. "How does that sound?"

---

"We seem to have a problem here, and I want solutions."

"They came out of nowhere, boss," said Ginger. "Too many for us to take on."

"Too many for you to take on? What are you, mice?"

"No, boss, Trig and me only just got away. They just burst into the club and pulled out knives and bats."

"And how many didn't get away?"

"Seven, boss."

"You left seven blokes to die? In my club? How would you like it if I left you to die? Maybe that's what I need to do?"

"This is out of control. They're going to slaughter us all," said Ginger. "They caught us off guard last night. They could hit somewhere else tonight. It's crazy. It's like they thought we deserved it. One of them actually said it was payback."

"Payback for what, Ginger? Why the sudden violence? I've been in this game my entire life, and believe me, it was nasty back in the eighties, but this is ridiculous. Where are the bloody police?"

"It's a retaliation, boss."

"A retaliation? Last thing I heard they killed Les, cut Jay's ears off, stole four kilos of coke, and blew up Tony. We haven't had time to retaliate ourselves yet."

"It's Bones, boss. Bobby Bones."

"Bobby Bones? What's he got to do with all this?"

"The Albanians hit his pub in Canning Town, burned it to the ground, his bookies as well."

"The one next door?"

"Yeah, the whole building was gutted."

"So what?"

"So Bones hit back, boss."

"He did what?"

"He retaliated, a bad one. One of our boys knows one of his boys, and well, cut a long story short, boss, Bones arranged for two van loads of blokes, all tooled up, to go in hard. Killed about twenty of them and then torched the gaff. A few got away with injuries and severe burns, and one is missing."

"Bones has him?"

"I think so, boss," said Ginger. "We reckon Bones has him tied up somewhere looking for answers. He's sick like that."

"Right, two things. Listen carefully."

"What's that, boss?"

"Tell me where I can find Bobby Carnell. We need to have a little chat. If he's going in hard, then we'll go in hard too. Make it public. In his pub is fine, he won't hit me there, not now. He needs me."

"What then, boss?"

"Well, once Bobby Bones and I have sorted out the Albanians, you and I will need to sort out Bobby Bones. He's cost me a lot of money so far, what with the missing coke and killing my men. I am *not* going to let him get away with it.

Rule number one, Ginger, make sure everyone knows who's in charge."

---

"Seven dead bodies?" said Frank. "Where's Stone? Tell me he wasn't one of them."

"No, sir," said Mills. "No word from Harvey. His phone is off."

"Where is he, Tenant?"

"He's at home by the looks of things," said Reg. "Tracker says he rolled in at four am."

"Is he making progress, Mills?"

"He's inside, that's all we know."

"Tell him to inform us when an attack is going down. I don't care how he does it. But if he goes on another job without telling us, I won't be the one opening the cell door to let him out, he's on his own."

"I will, sir."

"Let's piece this together," said Frank. "Bobby Carnell and his boys hit the Albanians in Highbury. Two hours later, the Albanians retaliate and hit a club in East London, a club that doesn't even belong to Carnell. Why did they hit there?"

"The guy with the ears, sir," said Melody.

"Mills?"

"He wasn't one of Bones' men. Nor was the guy in the car bomb. Harvey said the blokes he's in with haven't mentioned any of it."

"Go on."

"It makes sense. It's *not* Bones' pub. There's *two* firms," said Melody, like she'd just solved quantum physics. "Bones is going after the Albanians for torching his pub and bookies, but the Albanians think it's the other firm. They keep hitting back at the wrong people."

"Somebody is going to be awfully upset at that."

"Who else have we got?" said Melody. "Who runs the club?"

"Unknown. No grasses, no info," said Frank. "It used to be John Cartwright up until he went missing eighteen months ago. It's been quiet since."

"That's what we need to find out. That's the missing link," said Melody.

"Tenant, find out who owns the East Ham club that was torched last night."

"Already done, sir. It's a shell company, Conspectus Group."

"Who's on the board?"

"It's not public. That'll take some digging."

"So dig," said Frank. "Mills, find Stone, take him for a walk, have the chat. No more cocking about. I want to know who's running the other firm, if there is one."

"Sir, I've been thinking," said Melody.

"Go."

"Let's find out from Harvey what the state of play is with Carnell. Reg will do some digging on the other firm, but it's the Albanians that need stopping. It's them causing all the violence. But if we take away Carnell and the other firm, the Albanians will overrun the East End, and we'll have more than just a few fires to put out."

Frank thought on that for a moment.

"You're saying we should let the local firms take care of the Albanians? And then move in once it's just local firms left to deal with?"

"Unofficially, sir."

"That's a crazy idea," said Frank. "If the public got hold of that information, we'd be hung."

"Well, we'd need to act quick. If we can somehow get Harvey to manipulate the play, so the Albanians are outed fast, we can pull Harvey out and remove one or both of the local firms."

"We need at least one. As mad as it sounds, having a strong underground keeps the streets in order. But what we can't have is two strong players fighting over territory," said Frank. "Tenant, go dig. Mills, go find Stone."

# 7

## JUNKYARD CORRALL

HARVEY SAT ON HIS KITCHEN STOOL WITH HIS LAPTOP OPEN in front of him. He ran a search for Luan Duri, the name Aleksander had given up, but the results were hard to filter. There appeared to be many Luan Duris. Searches for Luan Duri London, Luan Duri criminal, and Luan Duri Highbury all produced virtually nothing of interest. He needed Reg's research power.

The previous night had reminded Harvey of his past life, not the pub fight, which had been unnecessary violence in Harvey's mind, but questioning Aleksander. Harvey enjoyed breaking people down. He'd tortured many people and found that no matter how hard the person was, they all broke in the end, and they all had some kind of story to tell.

Aleksander's story had been one that many British people wouldn't understand and couldn't empathise with. The average person wouldn't be able to imagine being forced to leave your family behind and venture into a scary new world with no money and no job and no skills. As soon as his feet hit British soil, he would have been on the run, an illegal immigrant. It was no wonder that people like him turned to a life of crime.

Harvey was looking for information that would take the Albanian boss down. The man was responsible for the deaths of a few men, probably many. There were a few that the team were aware of, but they'd need more on him. Harvey knew what was coming; he'd have to go and take a look, follow Luan Duri and find out for certain. If he could get his number, maybe Reg could get more information from it. If Harvey couldn't enable the team, there was no point being involved.

Aleksander hadn't been carrying a phone, but one of his men would be, and Luan's number would be stored on there. Aleksander had given up Luan's location, his office. All Harvey had to do was get close, and be patient.

Patience, planning and execution, the three pillars of Harvey's training with Julios. He knew it sounded almost military, but the approach worked. Harvey had used it dozens of times.

When Harvey was in his early teens, he'd found a police report of a boy he knew from his school days; a bully. The boy was on the run for sex offences which had immediately sparked Harvey's interest.

The boy who was on the run had also had run-ins with Harvey. He was a spiteful coward, and Harvey had slapped him about the playground when he found him picking on a small Asian kid.

When Harvey had read the report, he'd roamed the streets for a few weeks looking for him. He'd waited patiently in places where free food may be on hand, and in sheltered areas within the forest when it had rained. His patience had worked out well. Harvey found him lurking in the woods near his parents' home and dragged the kid deep into the trees where nobody goes. That had been Harvey's second kill, and it awoke a thirst. It wasn't a psychotic desire to torture and hurt people, it was a desire from deep within to avenge the young girls who, like his sister, had been abused.

Harvey had seen first-hand how lives are torn apart, families are destroyed, and how life is never the same for these people.

From then, Harvey had an outlet for the urges he had. He would pay attention to the news and other media. He would watch for court cases involving sex offenders, and he would be patient, he would plan his attack, then he would execute it. Over the years, Harvey had refined his methods of getting information out of people. He had honed the skills Julios had taught him about stealth and death. Harvey knew which parts of the body could be removed to provide the most pain, but not kill the victim. Harvey also learned how to research people, and when the internet became widespread, his research became even easier. He suddenly found targets in the outlying counties; he could open up his field of vision and target those who most deserved suffering.

What he needed to do now was to sit and watch Luan Duri. He needed to know where he went, who he was with; he needed to know his flaws, his weaknesses, his strengths.

Harvey stretched and rolled his head slowly from side to side. His body cried for a run, to limber up, to feel free again and breathe fresh air. He could still smell Aleksander's stale sweat.

The rain was loud against Harvey's kitchen window. It came in waves with the powerful gusts of wind. It wasn't a pleasant day for riding a motorbike. It was the type of day that never fully brightens up. The morning had been dark, the clouds had been low, and it had stayed that way until late morning. Harvey guessed it would stay that way until the evening too. But a dark day would work best for what Harvey needed to do.

Aleksander had said that Luan worked from a car breakers yard in Ilford, which was a ten-minute ride from Harvey's house in the dry. In the wet, it was maybe twenty minutes away. Harvey pulled up the satellite imagery view on his laptop. The yard backed onto the River Roding, a Thames tributary stood adjacent to the train tracks that led from London out to Essex and beyond. Harvey knew the area. The tracks were raised, and a small arched bridge beneath the tracks provided access to an industrial area. There were other yards around Luan Duri's, another car breakers and a building materials supplier. Harvey saw the pallets of bricks and lengths of timber and noted how clean it looked compared to the array of crumpled, broken and beaten cars that adorned the muddy breakers yard next door.

Harvey noted the small cabin that was central to the property. It was accessible via a direct mud track from the gates. Alternatively, as Harvey was aiming for stealth, he would use the maze of pathways that led between the cars. He would need to watch for dogs and maybe take something to deal with them. The yard was a great location for Harvey. It was out of the way so he could spend days watching if he needed to, he'd just hole up in an old car. It was also quiet so nobody would hear the screams of anybody he came across that compromised the operation.

Harvey closed his laptop and dressed in black cargo pants, his tan boots, white t-shirt, black hooded sweatshirt and leather jacket. He would be cold but would need to be agile, so he kept the layers to a minimum. Before leaving the house, he sent a message to Melody. *Got Alb boss' name, going for a recce.* He knew they would be watching him, so he didn't need to provide a location.

The ride to the junkyard was slow. The roads were slippery, flooded and busy with cars. Headlights reflected on the road's wet surface, and dark clouds loomed overhead. Harvey rode past the two huge gates to the yard. A trail of mud leaked from inside onto the pavement. The perimeter consisted of ten-foot brick walls, high enough to deter most people, but without barbed wire. Harvey parked his bike nearby between two cars that looked like they hadn't moved for some time. Before stepping off his bike, he checked his phone. Melody had replied. *We're watching you. Reg will update with more details.* Harvey stashed his helmet in the bike's back box and strode confidently along the path to the yard.

One of the gates was open, presumably for customers to drive in, so Harvey slipped inside and ducked behind a row of cars. If he was caught, he would just say he was looking for a part. It was typical for someone to find the right model of car before contacting the management to discuss removing and purchasing it. But nobody approached him.

The rain continued to lash down, which made listening for oncoming footsteps difficult. Harvey stopped by a stack of cars in the second row. The car still had seats, and they were dry. Each row of cars had two layers. The top layer seemed to be newer, and in better condition than the lower deck. Harvey climbed inside and pushed the seat all the way back, reclining it as far as it would go, then pulled an old tarp from the back seat over him. If someone were to walk past, Harvey would remain still under the dirty old cover. His view of the cabin was near perfect, save for the door pillars of the car in the first row.

Harvey settled in for the exercise in patience.

---

"I've got some bad news for you, boss," Ginger spoke into the phone.

"*More* bad news?" came the reply. "What is it now?"

"It's Malc, boss. He's gone missing."

"Missing? He's a full grown man, not a ten-year-old kid."

"I know, boss. But his missus called, said she hasn't seen him since yesterday morning."

"Is he on a bender? He likes a drink that man. We're not a missing bloody persons you know."

"Yeah, but it's weird. His car is still in the boozer car park with keys in the ignition, but his phone and wallet are gone. It's just not like him, boss. His missus is worried, and well, you know things are getting a little hot lately, maybe it's-"

"Maybe it's what, Ginger? The Albanians? Why would they take him?"

"Maybe payback for the bloke Carnell took?"

"Carnell? This is becoming a royal pain in the arse, Ginger. Have you found that little bastard yet?"

"Yeah, I'm trying to set a meetup, but apparently he's edgy right now. Our man has to pick the right time."

"The right time? Who's calling the shots here? Me, not Bobby Carnell. He's got two choices, meet me and discuss the Albanians or I'll add him to the list, and he knows that's a battle he won't win."

"Yeah, but he won't be pushed around, boss, even if it kills him. Even if he knows we outnumber them by more than double. He's a stubborn man."

"Where's he based? I'm not dicking about here, I'll go see him."

"Pied Piper, boss."

"The Pied Piper? What's he drinking in that dive for?"

"The Albanians burned his other local down. I guess all his other pubs are too far away for a swift half."

"Right, tomorrow night we're going to pay Bobby Bones a visit. Go see Malcolm's missus, give her some money. Tell her we'll find him. If she gets hysterical, tell her to shut up, or we won't bother, she can find him herself. Someone needs to take control here."

"Okay, I have some intel on the junkyard where Harvey is," said Reg, loud enough for everyone at headquarters to hear.

"What you got, Reg?" asked Melody. She was sitting in the reclining office chair with her feet on the desk and her laptop on her knees. The only noise in the open space was Jackson cleaning the van.

"I have the owner, his history, and his mobile. It's all we need to find out who he is and let us keep tabs on him."

Melody put her laptop down and walked over to Reg. "Show me."

"Right, Luan Duri, Albanian male, fifty-two years old. Formerly Albanian SHISH, which is the equivalent to the secret service. Retired with honours, then went missing when the new regime came into power. He's been hiding here for the past twelve years and is the owner of many businesses, mostly cash. Runs an export firm, probably stolen cars en-route to Albania, and a few junkyards officially. Unofficially, the crime squad have him linked to some pretty serious players in the city, and he allegedly runs a protection racket in North London, which is believed to include the Jumping Jack, the pub Harvey blew up last night."

"Hey, Harvey didn't blow it up," said Melody.

"Okay, it's the pub he dragged a two-hundred-and-fifty-pound man out of before throwing him into the back of a van," said Reg. "Which one is worse?"

"Do we have this Duri's number?" said Melody. "Where is he?"

"Have a guess?"

"Oh god, don't tell me, he's in the yard where Harvey is sat?"

"Bingo."

"Okay, *I'll* message Harvey, and tell him to get out. *You* keep tabs on Duri, and do some more digging," said Melody. She pulled her phone out, and it immediately beeped with an incoming message. *Albanians have a blindfolded man inside the junkyard. He hasn't got long. Do I engage or watch them kill him?*

Melody hesitated. Somebody's life hung in the air, and she needed to make the call. Save him and risk the operation or let him die? The man's death was by no means a guarantee of a successful mission, it would just allow the team more time.

"Sir," she called and waited for Frank's door to open. "Harvey is in the Albanian's junkyard. Reg has done some digging, and the guy is big time. Luan Duri, ex-secret service Albania. They have some guy blindfolded, and my guess is that it's not going to be a pleasant surprise."

"And you need *me* to tell *you* if you should compromise the investigation or let it play?"

"We should let it play, sir, I know we should. But will that come back and bite us in the-"

"We'll get a bigger bite if we expose Harvey now, Mills," said Frank. He eyed her and nodded. "Good call. Let it roll."

---

*Let it roll.*

Harvey read the message once then deleted it.

It was growing dark, and the rain was incessant. Harvey moved his feet and toes to keep the blood circulating. He was expecting the doors to open and the blindfolded man to be dragged out and dumped into the crusher. Harvey had seen that method of disposing of bodies before when he had worked for his foster father, John Cartwright. A junkyard was an asset for somebody dealing in stolen cars and dead bodies, making either one disappear was easy. Knowing a man with a junkyard was as good as knowing a man who ran a pig farm.

The lights were on inside the cabin, but the blinds were

pulled down. Harvey listened for the cries of the man being tortured but heard nothing above the rain hitting the metal roofs of the scrapped cars and splashing in the thick mud. A black Range Rover was parked outside the cabin alongside an old BMW, the only two working cars in the yard.

The sky fell quickly to a cloudy dark night, almost in the blink of an eye. The lights inside the cabin stared like lifeless eyes in the night. A train rumbled past on the overhead tracks a hundred yards away, carrying commuters heading home from a long day in the office, reading books and newspapers, listening to music and thinking about dinner. It seemed funny to Harvey that none of the people on the train knew what was about to take place a few hundred feet away.

The train's rumble faded away, and Harvey heard the first cry. The initial attack was always the worst, Harvey had found. The body isn't ready for it. It might be a finger chopped off with bolt cutters or it might be a toe. The methods generally get progressively worse, and the screams become less as the body's senses are numbed by the continuous attacks. Harvey typically preferred to use words to break a man; most men's minds were much weaker than their bodies. But if they refused, Harvey went straight for the ultimate pain. He wouldn't let the body become accustomed to small stabs of agony. It was far better to go straight in with the big guns.

He thought about Aleksander. Harvey had been prepared to light the fire, but in the end, he hadn't needed to. What Bobby Bones did with him afterwards was up to him. Harvey had done what had been asked of him and left them to it. Chances are that Aleksander had fallen foul of Bobby's twisted mind, and was minus a few fingers before a bag was thrown over his head.

A second cry sounded in the distance. It wasn't loud; it was muffled by the cabin walls and stacks of cars. But Harvey heard it clearly. It was a noise he'd heard a hundred times before.

The door opened, and the blindfolded man was kicked out onto the mud behind the Range Rover. He was naked. Two men stepped down beside him, and one more stood at the doorway. An older man had one hand in the pocket of a long jacket; the other held a cigarette to his mouth.

Harvey couldn't see what was happening, but he heard the words of the old man, spoken slowly and clearly. "Let him go."

The two men bent and picked the man up from the mud then kicked him along the grimy track towards the gate. They laughed as he staggered blindly in the dirt. Even from forty metres away, Harvey could see that he'd soiled himself. The blindfolded man felt his way along the row of cars. He trod carefully, walking barefoot on broken glass and sharp, rusty metal car parts.

Then the old man at the door whistled loudly. A few seconds later, two large German Shepherds came running from behind the cabin. The first saw the blindfolded man instantly and began to bound across the mud. The second was inches behind. The sound that followed was truly horrific. The snapping and snarling dogs made short work of the naked man, and after less than a minute, the screaming and crying fell silent. Only the sickening growls of the dogs tearing lumps of flesh from his body remained, along with the ever-present percussion of the rain on the metal roofs.

"Call them off," said the older guy. "Take his head, and deliver it to our friends." He pulled a long drag of his cigarette and flicked it into the mud before turning and closing the cabin door.

**8**

# TIGER TIGER

"HERE HE IS," SAID TREV WHEN HARVEY STROLLED through the door of the Pied Piper. "Where've you been? Playing football?"

Harvey looked at his boots and pants. They were caked in mud.

"Crazy day at work, Trev. How's tricks?" asked Harvey. "Please Lee." He caught the attention of the barman.

"Not bad, Gerry. Crappy weather though. Took me bloody ages to get here."

Harvey took the pint from Lee and turned to Trev. "Where's the boys?" he asked.

"They're most likely on their way. Old Doug can't go a night without a drink, probably stuck in traffic."

Harvey lowered his voice. "Any comeback?"

"Nothing, mate," replied Trev. "Surprising really, but just goes to show what pussies they are." He took a big mouthful of his drink and nodded at Lee for a fresh pint.

"Nothing?" asked Harvey. He leaned in closer to Trev. "We slaughtered them. Are you sure they haven't done anything?"

"Positive, Gerry. What's up with you?"

"Nothing's up. It's just, well, they're not really known for being forgiving, are they? I'm surprised *this* place is still standing to be honest."

"Maybe they got wind it was Bobby behind the attack, Gerry. Maybe they're busy running away."

"No, Trev. One thing I can guarantee you is that right now, they are *not* running away."

The door burst open, and a burst of fresh, cold wind hit Harvey. Doug and two other men walked in and closed the door behind them.

"Alright, lads?" said Doug, as he sauntered over to Harvey and Trev. "Blimey, it's brass bloody monkeys out there." He undid the buttons on his three-quarter-length leather coat and pulled off his scarf. "Please Lee," said Doug, catching the barman before he sat back down. "Here, Trev, you don't realise but you are standing next to a legend."

Trev looked around him with a confused look on his face. "Where? All I see is your ugly mug and this fella."

"You muppet. This fella here, Gerry." Doug slapped Harvey in the chest. "He's a nutcase, Trev." He leaned in and lowered his voice. "He had that fat Albanian singing in about ten minutes flat." Doug leaned away and took a long swig of his beer. "Ah, I needed that."

"What did he do?" asked Trev, and then turned to Harvey. "What did you do then, Gerry?"

Harvey didn't reply.

"Don't tell me. You look like a nasty bastard with that stare thing you've got going on. I reckon you pulled out his nails or something?"

"Nope," said Doug. "Try again."

Harvey remained impassive as the conversation turned into a game. It wasn't a game, it was people's lives, and could easily be either one of them when the investigation came to an end. Harvey had given thought to the case, and how it would actually be closed off. He'd need to wipe himself off every memory that knew his true identity. When the time came, either he had to step out of it or clean up those who saw him turn. There was no chance he'd be stepping away, but he'd need to keep the cleaning to a minimum. These people clearly had big mouths. Most of them would need to be closed for good.

"Alright." Trev studied Harvey. "If he didn't pull his nails, I'd say genitalia?"

"What?" said Doug. "That's schoolboy stuff."

"Well, I don't know. There's a thousand ways to get someone to talk."

"One last go," said Doug.

"Okay. I'm guessing Bobby was there?"

"Yeah, he enjoyed it very much."

"I reckon Gerry here peeled the skin off him, his legs, I'd say?"

"Nope, none of the above, Trev, my old mate," said Doug, looking at Harvey proudly. "You want to know?"

"Go on then, enlighten me."

"He spoke to him."

"You what?"

"Words, Trev. That's all he did was talk to him, had the fucking bloke in tears, even pissed all over the floor."

"Behave, Doug," said Trev. He turned to Harvey. "Is that right, Gerry?'

Harvey didn't reply.

"You hard bastard," said Trev. "Always the quiet ones, Doug."

"You ever done that sort of thing before, Gerry? I mean, it didn't look like your first time."

"First time, Doug. I must be a natural or something."

"No way was that your first time, Gerry. I've seen a few men get information out of someone, and never in my life have I seen someone so afraid of a man's word. It was electric, Trev. You could have cut the atmosphere with a spoon, mate."

"Are we ready for a surprise attack from the Albanians?" asked Harvey, changing the subject.

"What? They won't come nowhere near us now, mate. They know who we are and they're scared."

"Is that right?" asked Harvey. "Did they look scared to you?"

"Not really. But that was the heat of the moment, wasn't it?"

"Do you really think they'll let this go?" asked Harvey. "Are we going in for another go?"

"Yeah, I think Bobby is setting something up, a final kick up the arse. Why's that? You want in?" asked Trev.

Harvey turned to Trev. He eyed him and studied his gaunt face with its weak jawline. "Of course I want in. I want to finish what we started. I'm not going to be happily sitting here with a pint waiting for the Albanian mafia to recollect itself, storm in here and clean up. Now's the time to hit them."

"You're keen," said Doug.

"Yeah, well," said Harvey, "if there's one thing I hate more than a liar, it's a bully." Harvey turned and sank his beer. "Please, Lee."

"Well, the boss will be pleased to hear it," said Doug. "He'll be here soon, so be sure to voice your opinion why don't you."

"If he asks, I'll tell him."

"Don't just wait for him to ask, tell him what you just said, Gerry." Doug put his arm around Harvey's shoulder and walked him away from the others. "Listen, a geezer like you could do well with Bobby. He's solid, right? Been around for donkey's, hasn't he?" Doug stopped them both by the jukebox beside the washrooms. "What you doing for work, Gerry?"

"I'm just helping a mate out at the minute."

"That's code for unemployed, Gerry. You can't kid a kidder. Look at yourself, mate. Now, look at me. If a bird walks through that door right now, who's she going to take home? You in your dirty clobber, or me with my nice clean shoes and Armani jeans? Me, of course. Birds don't want to have to bath a bloke before she drags him into bed."

"What are you saying, Doug? It sounds to me like you're trying to push me into something here." Harvey let Gerry take control. The Harvey inside would have dragged the bloke outside and broken his arm just for touching him let alone insulting him.

"Easy, Gerry, no insult meant, mate. But you could do a lot worse than get a job with Bobby. He'll sort you out. You want me to have a word, or what?"

Harvey pondered on the question. Doug had played right into his hands.

"Yeah, alright then. What's involved? What's the pay like?"

"Gerry, mate, don't worry. You will be paid handsomely, and won't have to do much more than what you've done for him in the past couple of days. And if it's me that puts a word in, he's bound to agree. Did you see how impressed he was with what you did the other night?"

"Not really."

"Trust me, Gerry mate, you'll be fine. Look at you. I see loads of blokes come and go, and honestly, I can't remember the last time someone like you come along. You were made for this type of thing. I can't believe you've never done it before. Mate, you're a tiger, Gerry, a bloody tiger."

"Who's Dom then?"

"Dom? Oh, he's alright. He does all Bobby's legwork. Hard bloke, he earns well from Bobby."

"You reckon he'll be alright with it?"

"Mate, Bobby has got a boner in his pocket for people like you. Don't worry about Dom."

"What's he planning?"

"Who?"

"Bobby. You said he was planning something. What's he got in mind?"

"I'm not sure. I'm not privy to that kind of information until it's go time. Know what I mean?"

"Alright. When's he coming?"

"He's coming tomorrow night. Come down, have a word, he'll probably make you an offer on a job. Do well, and he'll give you more work. Keep your nose clean, and he'll have you on the payroll, doing his collecting or something."

"Alright, Doug. Thanks, mate. I'll be here tomorrow. I best be off now though, she's doing my nut in. Last thing I need is for her to walk in here tomorrow gobbing off when Bobby is here."

"Yeah, no worries. Take it easy, Gerry."

Harvey turned and opened the door. A stiff, cold wind blew around the pub, and all eyes fell on Harvey. He stepped out and heard Doug call after him. "Oy, Gerry." Harvey span around and saw Doug leaning out the pub doors. "Remember, you're a tiger, mate. A bloody tiger."

---

"He's got a big mouth, Melody," said Harvey. "Big mouths are dangerous in my experience. He means well but doesn't know when to shut up sometimes."

"Invincible gangster syndrome?"

"I think so. It's like they glorify the thing, the lifestyle, the violence, and for what? Easy money? That's all these people want is easy money and a sense of entitlement. Like because they're hard, they're somehow better than most. It's hard to keep my mouth shut sometimes, but Gerry plays along. He's a rookie, right?"

"Right."

Harvey threw the ball for Boon, who bounded across the grass and misjudged the ball's bounce. It bounced over him, and he caught it on the second drop before running back towards Harvey. The pair were walking through the open fields of Wanstead Flats. It was a large open area with a few small lakes and plenty of space to make sure they weren't overheard or seen.

The Flats were where Harvey had chosen to draw out Al Sayan, the terrorist who had rigged three black cabs with explosives six months previously. He had targeted the team, notably Harvey. So Harvey had gone to the largest open space close to the city and waited for Al Sayan to show his face. If Al Sayan had decided to try and kill Harvey in an explosion, the collateral would have been minimal.

"How's he doing?" asked Harvey.

"Boon? Yeah, he's good. He's a good fit for the team, you know? Reg loves him, and he's getting to know Jackson. I think he's a little wary of Frank, but the old man dotes on him. He mostly sits by my feet in headquarters."

Boon, the dog, had belonged to a man that Al Sayan had killed on the banks of the River Thames. It had been a long investigation, and ultimately, Harvey had pulled the Afghani terrorist off Tower Bridge into the water. They'd both been whisked away by the current and floated for miles downstream. When they eventually beached out in Essex, the dog walker had been in the wrong place at the wrong time. Harvey had stopped Al Sayan and taken the dog, rather than leave him on his own. The dog had been named Boon by Harvey, who then gave him to Melody as a present.

"So, what's the plan here?" asked Melody. "What happens next?"

"Doug the mouth thinks he can get me a job with Bobby Carnell."

"Okay, so a career move for Gerry," said Melody. "Does Frank know?" She smiled up at Harvey.

"Not really a career move, but Gerry is scratching for work and Carnell likes what Gerry does, so go figure."

"And once you're inside?"

"Well, once I'm inside and trusted, it'll be easier to start going in wearing a wire. Then we'll have enough on him to take him down clean."

"How long do you think that'll take?"

"Not sure, but things are moving. All this booze is killing me. I'm supposed to go the Pied Piper tonight to talk to him. Doug will make the suggestion and Bobby will give me a job or two to test me."

"Oh for god's sake, Harvey. You're going to get yourself in too deep."

"Relax, I know what I'm doing. I've lived and breathed this stuff all my life. I'm more experienced than Bobby's boys."

"But Gerry isn't. How's the legend holding up?"

"Simple. Gerry is out of work, not afraid to get his hands dirty, and can look after himself."

"What if they ask too many questions?"

"All part of the profile, Melody. Gerry doesn't tolerate questions, and they won't push him. They've seen what he's capable of."

"Need I ask?"

"Best not to, Melody."

"I saw, you know?"

"You saw what?"

"I saw you drag that man from the pub and load him into the van."

"Yeah, why didn't you stop to help me lift him?"

Melody laughed. "Oh, you know, I wasn't dressed for it."

"Is that right?" replied Harvey. "I thought you were goners when that pub blew. None of us had any idea that had been done."

"Worried, were you?"

"Thought we'd killed you when I saw the van come round the corner. It was like slow motion."

"I hear concern in your voice."

"Of course I was concerned, Melody. Imagine the grief I would have got from Frank."

Melody elbowed Harvey. "You'd have been sad, and you know it."

"Yeah, you're right. Who would I tell all my troubles to if you were dead?"

"You don't really tell me your troubles, Harvey. You don't really tell me anything. It's okay, I get it. I understand why you don't open up."

"What do you mean? This *is* me opening up."

"You want to know something?" asked Melody.

"Go on."

"When that pub blew, it felt like the whole van was in a ball of flame."

"That's pretty much what it looked like too."

"I loved it."

"You what?"

"Honestly, Jackson thinks I'm crazy. I laughed, it was exhilarating."

"You hung from a plane without a parachute six months ago, and you think *that* was exhilarating?"

"I think I was just pleased to be alive. But it was funny to see the look on Jackson's face."

"Yeah, welcome to the team, Jackson."

They walked slowly, and Melody kicked the grass. The

earth was soft from the previous day's downpour, and both their boots were soaked.

"You think about him much?" asked Melody.

Harvey knew Melody was referring to Denver, their teammate and friend who was killed by Al Sayan. "Yeah, I do as it happens. He was a nice bloke. You?"

"Every time I look at Jackson."

"Does Jackson seem out of place?"

"I'm not sure if it's because we're used to seeing Denver there, or, I don't know. But every time Jackson slides out from under the van, I expect Denver to grin at me."

"Time will tell, Melody. Think of the good stuff."

"I don't want to think about any of it, to be honest. I don't want to be reminded of Denver every time I look at Jackson. Is that wrong?"

"It's just your way of grieving, Melody. It'll get easier over time."

"How about the case?" asked Melody. "How do you see it playing out?"

Harvey let the words float around inside his head for a few seconds. "Something doesn't add up, Melody."

"You want to share that?"

"I watched that guy yesterday be dragged into the cabin in the junkyard. I heard his screams, and then once they got the answers they wanted, I watched the two German Shepherds tear him apart."

"Oh really, too much detail, Harvey."

"Then I heard Luan Duri tell his two boys to take the bloke's head and deliver it back as a message."

"Right?"

"I was in the pub last night, and not a dicky bird was said about it."

"Dicky bird?"

"Sorry, Gerry slips out sometimes. No-one said anything.

I even asked if the Albanians had retaliated and both Doug and Trev said they hadn't."

"Oh god, I keep forgetting you're not up to speed on things. It feels like you've been on holiday or something," said Melody. "Frank and I have a theory that there are two local firms involved."

"That's exactly what I was thinking."

"Carnell hits the Albanians, they strike back at the other firm and repeat."

"But who's the other firm?"

"No-one knows. Whoever it is has some loyal men. It's like they make a point of not being on the radar."

"So Bobby can expect a visit from both the Albanians and this other mob? Great," said Harvey.

"Frank wants to let it play."

"You what?"

"He wants to let the local firms take care of the Albanians, and then we'll take care of the local firms."

"There's going to be a lot of bloodshed."

"In his view, that's just thinning the numbers for when we step in."

"What does he want me to do?"

"Hang in there, do what you can, report back more often than you are, and stay alive."

Harvey nodded and stopped beside his bike.

"And what do you want me to do?"

Melody opened the door, and Boon jumped onto a blanket on the small back seat. She stepped closer to Harvey, reached up and put her arms around his waist. "I just want you to be careful."

# CLASH OF THE TITANS

"It's done, Luan," said Bardh. "I imagine right about now they will be discovering their friend."

"Good, they will retaliate. It's in their blood. And when they do, we will be ready."

"How many do we have?"

"We have thirty good men coming here right now, and another forty spread out across North London in case they strike there."

"Is thirty enough?" asked Bardh. "You saw what they did in the Jumping Jack."

"Those men were not carrying AK-47s. Trust me, when the local firm strikes here, it'll be the last thing they do." Luan paused to light a cigarette. "The crusher will be busy tonight." He smiled a cruel smile that showed his stained teeth.

"One of the men who escaped the fire is talking. He is in hospital still but able to talk. His skin has melted from his face, and his hair is gone. He is *vigan* now. A monster."

"He doesn't need to concern himself with his future. He will be taken care of."

"He spoke of one man, Luan. A dangerous man, far more talented than the other thugs."

Luan looked up at the man from his desk in the cabin. "Tell me more."

"He moved with precision, like a dancer. With each step, he will strike, and with each strike, he will kill."

"You sound scared, Bardh. Where are your balls?"

"I do not fear death, Luan, as you know. But we must destroy this man. He is trained. It was this man that took Aleksander, and if there is one man left standing at the end of this battle, it will be this man. He killed many of our men."

"Do we have a name for this *figure e dubluar?*"

"No, but if I am right, we will meet him soon. We have two men watching them, but until now, there has been no sign of this man."

"Do they keep him locked in a cage?" Luan smiled.

"He's special, Luan. He is a trophy."

"Then I want him found, and I want his head brought to me." Luan paused to take a drag on his cigarette. "With his balls in his mouth."

---

"Please, Lee," said Harvey. He was stood alone at the bar of the Pied Piper. Only the old man sat at the end of the bar where he always sat. The rest of the pub was empty.

"Quiet one tonight, Gerry," said Lee.

"Yeah, looks like it."

"Usually spells trouble."

Harvey didn't reply.

Lee set the pint down on the bar and leaned forward to Harvey. "So what's your story? You're not a local boy, are you?"

"We've had this conversation before, Lee."

"Yeah, you told me to mind my own business." Lee stood upright and folded his arms. "You know how long I've been running this pub?"

"I don't really care to be honest."

"Fifteen years. Fifteen years stood here behind this bar. Can you imagine that?"

Harvey didn't reply.

"The things I've seen, blimey, if these walls could talk. People come and go, Gerry. Always have and always will."

"I wish you'd go, and let me think."

Lee ignored Harvey's comment and carried on talking at him. "There's always been trouble in these parts, you know? But it was always amicable. It was always done with a bit of dignity, know what I mean?"

Harvey stared at the pub door. A car pulled in, and the headlights shone briefly through the glass.

"Old school firms, now they had class, Gerry. Don't get me wrong, they'd cut your face off for looking at them the wrong way. But if you were on the right side of them, they'd take care of their own. It's not like that these days. It's every man for himself, dog eat dog. Sure, these boys all get along, they're on the same firm. But when push comes to shove, and someone has to go down, it'll be a scramble for the top and those at the bottom will be trodden on and forgotten."

Car doors slammed, and men's voices could be heard outside.

"Take my advice, Gerry. Don't get involved. You aren't the first one to get caught up in the bother, but get out while you can. You seem like a nice bloke, bit hard and a bit protective, that's fair. But do yourself a favour, turn away and don't look back."

The doors burst open, and Doug, Trev and two others walked in. "Oy oy, Gerry, you're keen tonight."

"How's it going, Doug? Trev?" Harvey shook the men's hands.

"Yeah, not bad, Gerry," said Doug. "Please, Lee." He made a circle with his hand indicating that he wanted a round of beers for everyone.

"What's new?" asked Harvey.

"Oh, this and that, Gerry. The wife is still gorgeous, and the dog's breath smells. Actually, no, that's the wrong way round." Doug laughed at his own joke, slapped Harvey on the back, and picked up a beer from the bar. "And one for yourself, Lee, my old son."

"Cheers, Doug," replied Lee.

"Listen, Gerry, remember what I said last night? Bobby is coming down, he's got some news. Me and Trev reckon he's going to tell us what his plans are with the Albanians. I reckon we're going in hard, crack a few skulls."

"Sounds like fun," said Harvey. "Any idea what time he's getting here?"

"Any minute, mate. Just listen hard, and I'll talk to Dom to make sure word gets put his way, see if we can't get you a bit of work."

"Nice one, Doug. Appreciate it."

"No problem, mate."

The door opened, and more men walked in. Hard types, thought Harvey. Shaved heads, tattoos, gold sovereign rings and not one piece of un-scarred skin on show. They looked like the men that John used to have working for him in the eighties, the men that would be hanging around the house when Harvey was a child. Doug nodded at them. Harvey looked away for two reasons. Nobody liked to be stared at when they walk into a pub, and there was a small chance one of them may recognise Harvey if they had worked for John at any point in their criminal careers.

The TV was turned on and the football game was playing.

Harvey pretended to be absorbed by it, but actually had no idea what was happening. He listened to the banter around him. He'd never learned how to deal with banter; he'd never been in the situation where allowing a man to insult you for any reason, even humour, was acceptable. Harvey had spent a large part of his life being invisible, barely existing. Anybody that had known him had known how dangerous he was and was highly unlikely to offer an insult, even in jest.

The pub was getting fuller. Gradually over the next hour, more men filtered in, slapped friends on their backs and bought beers for everyone they knew then insulted them. Harvey sipped his pint and observed the play.

When Bobby 'Bones' Carnell walked into the room, preceded by Dom, the bar fell virtually silent.

Bobby walked to the bar where a scotch and soda was placed in front of him and a pint for Dom. The noise crept back up to its original volume.

Harvey moved along to the end of the bar and stood behind a column in a relatively empty space. There was a small booth there that was hardly used. Harvey sat down with his back to the wall, which gave him a clear view of the front doors. He pulled his phone out and messaged Melody. *BBC in PP. Will update.*

Harvey watched the dynamics of the firm. He knew that Bobby had more men than those in the pub. These were just the core, Bobby's most loyal men. There were about forty of them in total, plus maybe the same again not in attendance.

Harvey saw more headlights pull into the car park, four cars, judging by the waves of light that shone through the opaque glass windows. Harvey finished his drink and sat with an empty glass.

He watched the doors open, and six men walked in. They were all big guys with leather jackets, stony stares, and matching scars. The room fell silent. From where Harvey was sat, he could see Dom push himself off the bar where he'd been leaning and stride through the centre of Bobby's men.

"Is there a problem, boys?"

The new men stood silently either side of the door, three per side.

"Are you fucking deaf or something?"

The room was deathly silent. Lee flicked the TV off and led the old man around the bar out of harm's way. He limped around carrying his pint and disappeared into the back function room.

Then two things happened that shocked Harvey.

The door opened again, and before Harvey had even seen who it was, he saw the heads of Bobby's men tilt backwards to look at the giant man. One massive leg came into view, and then the barrel chest and thick jaw of Adeo Parrish. Harvey was transfixed. He was hidden in the shadows and couldn't be seen by the big man. Adeo was Julios' brother. Harvey had only met him six months previously during a strange series of events in which their paths had crossed. Adeo had been Stimson's bodyguard during the terrorist attack that had killed Denver and nearly killed Harvey. Adeo was the only one to have gotten away and *would* recognise Harvey if he saw him.

Harvey ran through his options. He was in a pub with more than fifty men between him and the doors, all of whom would slaughter Harvey if they found out he was working with the police and wasn't actually called Gerry.

He could take them on, but he knew that the odds were stacked heavily against him. He could shoot his way out, not a brilliant solution by any means. As he only had a magazine of fifteen in his Sig P226, he wouldn't get halfway through the firm before someone got lucky. Or he could hang onto every little bit of hope he could conjure up. But Harvey wasn't feeling lucky.

Adeo stepped to one side of the doors. His mass seemed

to fill the room. The doors opened once more, and as if in slow motion, all eyes fell back to the door. A shiny brogue stepped through, and then the calm, confident swagger of John Cartwright.

He stopped and let the door bang shut behind him. Then, in the thick, gruff but articulate tone that Harvey remembered so well, he said, "Which one of you is Bobby Carnell?"

---

"I am. Who's asking?"

Bobby's reply sounded light, weak and dulcet compared to the harsh grumble of John Cartwright's cacophonous voice.

"Do I really need to answer that?" replied John.

"Cartwright?"

"Mr Cartwright to you."

"And to what do we owe the pleasure, Mr Cartwright?" said Bobby, trying to sound large and confident in front of his men.

"Thought we'd have a chat. You can get your pets to stand down. We haven't come looking for a tear up," said John. "Yet."

The two men eyed each other with distrust. Harvey saw the men in Bobby's ranks discreetly sliding coshes and knives out of their waistbands.

"Alright, boys," said Bobby. "Stand down."

He turned back to John. "It's most irregular for men like you and me to step into another man's pub. But, seeing as you're here, let's keep it civil. What're you drinking?"

"I'll take a brandy, Remy Martin. Three ice cubes. No more, no less."

Lee heard the order and began to pour the drink. The two men moved towards the bar, and Bobby's guys opened up the room. Men still drank, but nobody dared talk. Everyone was on high alert, waiting for a move from one of Cartwright's men.

"So, what's the topic, Mr Cartwright?" asked Bobby. "What exactly is it we're discussing?"

"Ginger?" called Cartwright.

A bald man with a red-haired goatee beard stepped away from the door and walked up to John. John nodded at him. Ginger pulled a canvass bag with a drawstring up and sat it on the bar. He began to pull the strings open.

The front ranks closed in, but John Cartwright held his hand up. "Easy, boys, calm down. It's not a weapon."

Ginger opened the drawstring and reached inside. He lifted his hand and pulled the bag away from the bottom to reveal a man's severed head. He dumped it on the bar in front of Bobby.

"Cheers, Ginger," said John, and Ginger moved back to his place by the door.

"Pretty," said Bobby and gestured with his head at the one that sat on the bar looking at him.

"One of my men," said John.

"Well? Isn't he looking for it or something?" replied Bobby. "I understand, John, that you are a grandfather in this world. I know you've been around since the good old days. But you know what? *That* makes *this* even worse." Bobby took a swig of his drink. "You come in here unannounced with half a dozen armed men." Bobby stared at each of the six men by the doors. "You're all carrying, aren't you?" Nobody replied. Bobby turned back to John. "They're all carrying, right?"

John gave a small shrug.

"And you bring this goon," said Bobby, gesturing at Adeo who stood far above any man in the pub. "What are you feeding him? Horses?" Bobby took another mouthful of his drink and gestured at Lee to pour another. "So you can see my problem, John. This is borderline taking liberties, mate."

"Considering this is your turf, I'll disregard your tone with me that once. But mark my words, Bobby Carnell, if you ever talk to me like that again, I'll cut you down myself." John spoke calmly and easily, unafraid even though heavily outnumbered. Harvey looked on with familiar admiration for John's control and presence. The man was born to do what he did.

John Cartwright had been missing for two years since he'd made a deal with Harvey. The deal was that Harvey was to kill the number one rival crime family. Their leader, Terry Thomson, was one of the most feared criminals Harvey had ever known. His habit of feeding live people to his pet two-hundred-and-fifty-pound hogs had been common knowledge in the organised crime world. In return for the kill, Harvey would receive the name of the man that raped his sister, the first name on Harvey's list. John had left Harvey to do what he needed to do and hadn't been seen since.

Until now.

"The reason I'm here, Carnell, is simple. A little birdie tells me you've been having trouble with the Albanians?" John swirled the three ice cubes in his glass.

"Nothing we can't handle," replied Bobby. "Isn't that right, boys?"

A dull chorus of agreements emanated from the group of men.

"Is that right?" said John. He cocked his head and lifted an eyebrow.

"We've got them on the run, haven't heard anything from them in days. All mouth, no trousers I believe is the expression."

"Is that right?" said John again. "Has it ever occurred to you that they aren't very bright, Carnell? One English bloke is the same as the next English bloke."

"What do you mean?"

John nodded at the gruesome head on the bar. "You think that just fell off, do you?"

"No."

"How do you think it happened to come apart from the rest of him?"

Bobby sighed. "Albanians?"

"Correct, Carnell. Malcolm here was kidnapped from outside one of my pubs, taken somewhere and decapitated."

"Yeah but-"

"Do not interrupt me, Bobby Carnell, when I am talking."

Harvey had strong memories of John's hatred of being interrupted and recognised the structure of the sentence.

"I also lost a good man, and a dear friend, when the Albanians jumped their motor. They cut the other man's ears off, Bobby. Also, my number two, a very loyal man, Bobby, was blown up outside the hospital. And finally, I lost one of my clubs and *seven* more men. One of my favourite clubs, Bobby." He paused to take a drink then nodded at Lee for another. "Now you tell me what exactly you are going to do about it because it seems like every time you and your band of merry men here attack the Albanians, it is me who is taking the flack for it. And you know, I can strike back, Bobby. I could destroy them and you. But I value my men, they're loyal. So why should they put their lives on the line for something that you did, Bobby? Answer me that."

"We didn't know they were going after you, John," said Bobby quietly. "Sorry about your men." Bobby looked around the room at all the faces. He knew them all by name; he respected all of them.

"How would you have known?" said John. "But you do now, so tell me what the answer is."

"Seems to me like the Albanians have wronged us both, John."

"I'd agree with that statement."

"So we both owe them."

John nodded.

"Why don't we team up? I've got seventy or eighty men. You can pull that together I'm sure. Let's finish it."

John nodded again. "Who's your best man?"

Bobby looked around the room again. A few of the faces stood tall, pumped their chests out and looked at Bobby for recognition. A few others seemed to sink back into the crowd. "Where's the new boy? Gerry?"

# BEAST ON FORM

"REG, IT'S MELODY."

"Oh hey, Melody. It's been all of two hours since I saw you. How's things?" said Reg in a mock female tone.

"No time. I need you to scramble Jackson and pick me up."

"Okay," said Reg. "Let me guess, Harvey?"

"How long?"

"Thirty minutes."

"I'll be waiting outside."

Melody disconnected the call and re-read the message from Harvey. It was the first time Harvey had ever sent a message of this sort and Melody was worried for him. *In PP, BBC here. JC and Adeo just arrived!*

It had taken Melody a few minutes to work out who JC was. She knew Adeo from the Al Sayan incident, and that spelt trouble. Adeo had been there when the team had caught Stimson. He knew that Harvey was working with the police, and that left Harvey in an extremely uncomfortable position. But when she had put the name John Cartwright to the initials, her heart sank.

John wouldn't know that Harvey was undercover. But the risk of him spotting Harvey and blowing his cover as Gerry would raise immediate flags in Bobby Carnell's firm. Harvey would be questioned, and the trust he'd built up would be gone.

She changed back into her work clothes, cargo pants and boots, a tight-fitting t-shirt and short leather jacket, then filled a flask of hot water. It was going to be a long night, and she liked to be prepared. But mostly it was to kill time and stop her mind wandering while she waited for Reg and Jackson.

The van pulled up after twenty-five minutes, and Melody climbed in, barely giving Jackson time to fully stop the van. "Go. Pied Piper."

She turned to Reg in the back. "Do we have him on screen?"

"We sure do. He's still there. So is Bobby Bones and a few other numbers in the network we've been building up."

"Put your foot down, Jackson. If it kicks off, I want to be there."

"Melody," said Reg, "if it kicks off, you can't go in guns blazing. Harvey knew the risk."

"I want him to know we're here for him."

"He knows, Melody."

Melody climbed into the back with Reg and pulled open a peli-case. She assembled a Heckler and a Koch MP5 and slotted the scope on top.

"What exactly are you planning to do with that?"

"You know what they call this?"

"A gun?" said Reg. He'd been trained in firearms but under duress and out of necessity. His choice of weapons was a blaster on his zombie-killing video game.

"Barking dog, Reg," said Melody, as she snapped a magazine into place. "You know why?"

Reg was silent.

"You'll know when you hear it. A few bursts with this and they'll scatter."

"Leaving us to pick up the pieces of Harvey," said Reg.

Melody looked Reg in the eye in the darkness of the van. She saw a glimmer of moisture in his eye and knew that he was using humour to cover his anxiety.

"Let's hope not, Reg."

---

Harvey stood up and stepped forward into the throng of men, who parted and made way for him to pass through. Some eyed him cautiously; others looked at him with contempt. They were perplexed at how a newcomer to the firm had suddenly earned the title of best man.

Harvey ignored Adeo, but out of the corner of his eye, he saw the recognition. His eyes widened, and mouth fell open, but to his credit, he remained silent. John had his back to Harvey and was drinking his drink. He looked up and caught Harvey's stare in the mirror behind the optics in the bar. John remained motionless.

"So, you're Gerry, are you?"

Harvey didn't reply.

"Gerry what, Son?" John spoke the last word slowly and decisively.

Harvey ignored the hidden greeting. "Sloan."

"Gerry, this is John Cartwright, show the man some respect, eh?"

"It's okay Bobby. He looks like a bright boy, he'll learn some manners," said John. He remained with his back to Harvey, swirling the ice cubes in his drink as he'd always done. "Bobby here tells me you're his best boy. Is that right?"

Harvey didn't reply.

John stood silent for a moment.

"If I was to tell you to do a job for me, Gerry, would you do it?"

"Tell? Or ask?" Harvey had seen the trick question coming from his foster father. John hated weakness; his favoured men had all earned John's respect by standing up for themselves. They had never been rude, but they hadn't been pushed around either.

John nodded.

"Sorry, John, he's new," said Bobby.

John raised his hand and shook his head.

"If I told you that we have a problem with the Albanians, and I needed someone to take them out, would you be willing to help?"

"If you asked nicely, John."

Bobby slapped his forehead in disbelief. His eyes were popping out of his gaunt face.

"Okay, I'll ask nicely, Gerry."

"Probably then," said Harvey. "But I'd do it on *my* terms, and *my* terms only."

"I'm really sorry, John," started Bobby. "Dom, take him-"

"Leave him be," said John. He turned with his drink to face Harvey. Harvey stared at the old man's face. He hadn't seen him for two years, but he hadn't changed much; he looked older, but his hard features bore the aged skin well. He was clean shaved as he always was. Old school habits.

"What might those terms be, Gerry?"

"I go in with your best man."

"*My* best man?"

Harvey didn't reply.

"You think the two of you can pull it off?"

A murmur built up among the men, then quietened when Harvey turned to Adeo.

"Him."

John downed his drink and placed the glass symmetrically on a cardboard coaster that sat on the bar.

"When?" asked John.

"Now. We leave now and come back when it's done. These blokes can all go home to their wives and kids."

"What? And what do expect us to do while you're gone, Gerry?" asked Bobby. "Twiddle our thumbs and wait for the heroes to come home?"

Harvey didn't reply.

"And if you don't come back?" asked John.

"I'll be back," said Harvey.

---

Harvey drove. Adeo filled the rest of the space in the front of the BMW that Dom had given to Harvey. They drove in silence. Neither one acknowledged the identity of the other.

Harvey felt his phone vibrate in his pocket, a message from Melody probably. He saw the square outline of the van in the rear-view mirror and made sure that Adeo hadn't spotted him checking. The team were a card up Harvey's sleeve, and would likely come in handy in the very near future.

They pulled off the A406 North Circular Road and slipped into the back streets of Ilford. As they passed under the railway bridge, Harvey pointed out the yard on the left.

They parked a few hundred meters further on than the gate. Parking in the evenings was difficult; commuters were coming home from work and spaces went like gold dust. Harvey reversed into a spot, using the car's parking sensors to get into the tight space.

He killed the engine.

"Before we go in, I want to make one thing clear."

Adeo looked back at him with his hand on the door handle.

"We do this my way. That's the only way we'll get back out again. If you deviate, you're on your own."

"You think you're better than me?"

"I was trained by the best."

"There's one thing you haven't considered, Harvey Stone," said Adeo as he pushed the door open and heaved his mass out of the car. Harvey climbed out and leaned on the car roof opposite the big man. They stood face to face. For Harvey, it was like seeing Julios stare back at him with his unemotional eyes and stern frown. "Who do you think trained me?"

The team's VW van passed behind Adeo as the two men stood facing each other across the car.

"The junkyard is set out in rows," began Harvey. "The cabin is in the centre. The crusher is behind it. There's rows of cars on the left, rows of cars on the right, rows of cars at the back and front with a space leading from the gate to the cabin. Plenty of places for them to be hiding. Luan Duri is the main man, old guy in a long jacket, smokes too much. I don't know how many there will be."

"You've been here before?" said Adeo, his brow furrowed.

"You think I'd come here without a plan?"

"So much of Julios in you."

"I'll take that as a compliment."

"Are we going over the wall?" asked Adeo.

"If the gate is locked, yes. Can you handle that?"

Adeo didn't reply.

The pair walked off towards the gates. The road was quiet, and they were blessed by a dark night. Harvey checked the parked cars all along the front to make sure there weren't any lookouts. All the cars were empty.

The gates were wide open.

"Keep walking," said Harvey. The pair marched past the

open gates and slipped down the side of the property between the yard and the embankment that led up to the train tracks.

"That was a trap," whispered Harvey. "Last time I was here, only one gate was open. It's like they're expecting us to walk in guns blazing."

Harvey pulled an old wooden pallet from a deep puddle and stood it beside the wall. Without a word, he climbed up, reached up to the top of the wall and pulled himself up. He lay on the wall and looked back down at Adeo.

"One last thing," whispered Harvey. Adeo had one foot on the pallet and was preparing to pull himself up. "I hope you like dogs."

Harvey flashed Adeo a warning smile and lowered himself down to the floor.

He pulled his knife from its sheave on his belt and took the time to listen for any movement. There were voices in the open space near the cabin. Several men were huddled around a fire inside an old oil drum like hobos.

Harvey felt rather than heard Adeo land behind him; the ground shook slightly. But as Harvey turned, Adeo stood upright. It hadn't surprised Harvey, Julios had been as big as Adeo and had been far more agile than he looked.

Harvey made a circle motion with his hands, indicating to Adeo that they would split and work the perimeter, meeting up on the far side of the yard. Adeo gave an imperceptible nod and turned away from Harvey.

Harvey watched him for a few seconds. It was like having Julios back. Harvey had never been afraid of anything. But for the twenty years he'd been trained by Julios, he'd worked with him for close to fifteen of them, and there was a certain level of comfort knowing the big guy had his back. Working alone had never been an issue, but having a solid and reliable partner was invaluable and mitigated much of the risk.

Harvey began to make his way around the ring of cars. He checked inside every one he came across and looked through to the next row if he could. Inside the cars made an ideal place for someone to wait, as he had done himself just two days previously. There was some banging in the distance, metal on metal, followed by a long scrape of something heavy being dragged across concrete, like a car part.

Harvey found the first guard napping on the passenger seat of an old Ford Escort. Harvey effortlessly flicked the tip of his blade into the man's neck and severed his windpipe. He left a wound less than an inch long, and the man woke immediately, fighting for air and drowning in his own blood. Harvey held the man's mouth closed until his lungs filled and he stopped moving.

Harvey continued on his walk. He stood at the back wall of the property behind the cabin and the crusher, and saw the open cage where the two German Shepherds lay. He crept silently; he was out of sight of the dogs but smelled cigarette smoke. The hushed voices of two men came from behind the next car. Harvey waited, watching them talk quietly. They were big men, but relaxed and off guard.

Harvey made a plan.

He found a small steel nut on the floor and tossed it behind the men. They both span around. Harvey watched as one signalled for the other to remain where he was and be quiet. Then the first one slipped away. He hadn't taken five steps when Harvey's garrote slipped over the man's head, and Harvey silently dragged him into the shadows.

The first man crept back along the wall towards the corner where Harvey stood. Harvey saw his vague shadow and heard his heavy boots.

"Hello?"

Harvey could smell the cigarettes on the man's breath.

*"Kush eshte atje?"*

The big man came around the corner slowly and hesitantly. Harvey slipped around the car and came up behind him. When the man's foot kicked the soft body of his friend, he bent to see what it was. He then stood up and took a deep breath ready to alert everybody. Harvey's knife came from behind him. One slice across his throat and the big man fell to his knees, choking on his own blood.

Harvey left the two dead men in a pile in the shadows and made his way quietly along the wall, where Adeo met him.

"What took you so long?" whispered the big man.

Harvey ignored the comment. He knew that if Julios had trained him, Adeo would understand that the delay was due to obstacles. Given that Adeo had taken nearly the same time to make half a circuit, Harvey guessed that he had also come up against only two men maximum.

Harvey signed to move into the next ring of cars and complete another half circuit.

They went back the way they had each came to maintain familiarity. But the second ring of scrap was far more challenging without the benefit of the shadow the wall provided. Harvey felt he could be seen through the windows of cars in the inner circles.

He moved slowly. His eyes picked up the slightest movement, the flutter of a discarded wrapper on the floor as the breeze blew across it, the flap of a loose seat belt. Harvey was directly behind the cabin once more when movement in the corner of his left eye stopped him in his tracks.

One of the dog's ears had stood up. It was lying down, relaxed, but one ear was raised and turned like a satellite towards Harvey. He remained dead still. Voices came from near the cabin as two men walked loudly towards the spot where Harvey had dropped the two smokers.

The dog's head turned and his eyes locked with Harvey's. He didn't move. It stood and walked briskly out of its open cage and turned in Harvey's direction. Its ears were pinned back as it closed in.

The two men came briefly into view between two cars then disappeared into the shadows.

Harvey heard the low guttural growl of the dog as it approached with more urgency. But Harvey stood his ground. He held his knife by his side ready to strike the dog between its front legs if it attacked.

He knew Shepherds, and if it had been trained well, it would go for his arm or throat, more likely the throat. It would use its weight to bring Harvey down then sink its teeth into the soft tissue of his neck.

The other dog moved in behind the first. Both dogs stood in front of Harvey. Their hackles were up and their ears pinned back. The first dog was the alpha. The second would follow the first dog's lead. Harvey stared at the alpha, unafraid. The showdown lasted thirty seconds, no more. Then the alpha broke eye contact, and its ears dropped. The second followed suit.

Harvey was now lead dog.

He dropped to his haunches, and the dogs came to him like they were old friends.

Harvey stood and shooed them away. Then, before he knew it, they pounced behind him and pinned a large Albanian man to the ground. The man struggled as the lead dog tore into his throat. He punched out, but both dogs held on, and he finally gave up. His body fell limp, and the dogs sat by their quarry.

Harvey stared the first dog in the eye and held its cold gaze. Its mouth was black with blood in the dark night, but there was one more man in the shadows somewhere. Harvey stood motionless and let the movement come to him. The shadow on the car in front grew darker as somebody moved past very slowly.

The dogs were too noisy when attacking, so Harvey had them sit and stay using two movements of his hand to the more aggressive of the dogs. The second followed suit. They sat and watched Harvey slip silently behind the man and pull the steel wire cable tight around his neck. The man was strong and fought back with defensive judo moves that Harvey recognised and countered. All the while, he maintained pressure on the steel wire. The large Albanian managed to use his bulk to turn and face Harvey, so Harvey leaned back and slammed his forehead into his nose. Dropping the wire, he snapped the man's head to one side, who dropped like a stone at the feet of the German Shepherds.

Harvey signed for the dogs to stay and slipped into the shadows between the two cars. Adeo was waiting for him again and stepped out of the darkness when Harvey approached. This time there was no jibe at the delay, and Harvey saw Adeo's blood-stained hands.

There was one more row of cars to get around before the cabin.

Adeo stepped closer to Harvey and ducked down beside him behind the cars. He signed with a bloodied hand that he'd seen a risk. Harvey looked back at the open space in front of the cabin. The men had set up a tripod-mounted flamethrower either side of the alley of cars that led from the gates to the cabin. One man stood on either side, ready to incinerate anybody that came up the alleyway.

The flamethrowers didn't pose a problem to Harvey or Adeo. But from where the men stood, they wouldn't get close to the cabin without being spotted.

"How many men inside the cabin?" whispered Adeo.

Harvey shrugged. Adeo leaned in close to Harvey. "Once we're inside that cabin, there'll be no more hiding. We'll have seconds to take them out."

Harvey shook his head. "Too risky." He chanced a glance

around the edge of the car in front to make sure the men were still there, and then ducked back to Adeo. "We need to draw them out. We have the advantage out here."

"And how do you plan on doing that?"

Harvey stood, drew his Sig from his waistband and stepped into the open space. He fired twice, one round in each of the men's heads.

## TWO DOGS

"WAS THAT GUNFIRE?" ASKED MELODY, COCKING HER HEAD to one side.

"I don't know," said Reg. "It's a pretty industrial-"

"Shhh," said Melody. She was listening for more fire.

"You asked," said Reg.

"Oh this is killing me," said Melody with her head in her hands. Her MP5 lay across her lap ready to go at a moment's notice. "Reg, can you get Frank on the loudspeaker?"

Within a few seconds, the van filled with the sound of a ringing phone.

"Tenant, what's the news?"

"Sir, it's me. You're on loudspeaker," said Melody.

"Go on."

"It's just an update, sir. Harvey has been inside the yard for more than thirty minutes."

"Any action?"

"We just heard two gunshots."

"You thought we heard gunshots," said Reg.

"Did you or didn't you hear gunshots, Mills?"

"Ninety-nine percent sure, sir."

"Same gun?"

"Definitely. But I couldn't hear it clear enough to make out if it was a Sig."

"Spacing?"

"Double tap, of that I'm sure."

"Then it's Stone. Those Albanians will be using AKs, forty-sevens or seventy-fours."

There was a silence while Frank made a decision.

"Sit tight, wait for the chaos. If I know Stone like I think I do, the whole place will erupt any minute."

"Copy that, sir."

"Mills?"

"Sir?"

"Thanks for the update. Make sure our boy gets out in one piece." Frank disconnected the call.

---

The door of the cabin was kicked open, and two men ran out brandishing AK-74s. They spat a few rounds in Harvey's direction then ducked behind some cars. Harvey didn't take the bait. Instead, he dipped back down to Adeo.

"The surprise is up, but this isn't over until Luan Duri is face down in the mud," said Harvey.

Adeo nodded and stood. He pulled his own weapon from a discreet holster beneath his arm. He slid the action back and let it slide forward, collecting a round on its way.

Harvey ran between the cars to the far wall behind the cabin. Adeo ran in the opposite direction. Taking a quick glance back toward Adeo, Harvey saw him disappear around the corner near the gates. Harvey moved off towards the two men he'd dropped earlier.

Voices rang out in the night, confused shouts in Albanian, along with the occasional bursts of automatic fire. These weren't trained men. If they were, they wouldn't be shouting. A man was framed in the window of a car; he was waiting in the shadows. Harvey took him down with the butt of his Sig then finished the job with a swipe of his knife through his throat. He knelt beside the dying man, looked around, then stood to make his way towards the rear of the cabin. He caught sight of something in the corner of his eye and turned to find the two dogs sat perfectly still, exactly where he had left them. Harvey gave a light whistle, and the dogs ran to his side. He chanced a glance up to the cabin window and peeked inside. The back of the old man's head was in clear view. He was sat at a desk giving orders to another guy with tattoos.

Harvey checked around him; he was alone. He turned back and raised his weapon. Then the lights went out, and the sound of chairs scraping along the cabin's thin floor came through the walls.

Adeo, Harvey thought. He must have tripped the switch. Harvey had had a clean shot, but couldn't risk missing now by firing into the darkness. He moved to the corner of the cabin. A roar of automatic fire came from less than ten metres away, but Harvey couldn't see its source. He stole a quick look around the side of the cabin and saw a man firing from the hip like he was in was a movie, walking backwards out of Adeo's range. Harvey fired once and took the man down. He considered taking the AK but thought better of it. They were too cumbersome, and he intended on being out of the junk-yard in less than two minutes.

From where Harvey stood, he saw the gates and Adeo's massive shadow moving closer to the open space. One Albanian had dragged his friend away and now manned one of the flamethrowers. Harvey took careful aim, released a single round and hit the five-foot-tall orange gas bottle directly. The bottle exploded with such force that before the flames had taken form, Harvey saw the man being blown like a leaf in the breeze towards the cabin.

More shouts filled the silence between short bursts of the automatic weapons. Car lights lit the alleyway to the gates where Adeo was waiting, and the roar of a powerful engine overshadowed the chaotic shouts. A small part of Harvey hoped it was Melody with her MP5. But it wasn't the team. It was a BMW that tore through the gates and aimed directly at the massive bulk of Adeo. The big man had no time to react. He threw himself onto the bonnet of the car, lifting his legs clear of the bumper, and slammed into the windscreen. He bounced over the roof and landed heavily in the mud. The car slid to a halt as Adeo rolled on his back and clutched his chest.

Harvey slipped back into the shadows. The dogs followed.

The cabin spewed out men, more than Harvey had imagined had been in there. He couldn't understand the language of the shouting, but he got the gist. The gates were slammed and locked, and he watched as Adeo was dragged unconscious into the cabin and the door was closed.

Men began to spread out, searching the grounds for Adeo's accomplices. The lights came on in the cabin, and the ground around him lit up. He pointed to the cage and gave a verbal command to the dogs. "Go." The dogs trotted off and lay down on the ground. By the time they had turned to watch him, he had slipped further into the depths of the ranks of cars.

Harvey shivered; the adrenaline was wearing off. Footsteps came from his left. The Albanians were more confident in their search now and they walked in pairs. Harvey stepped out just as two men drew close. He slotted one in the neck and jammed his finger into the eye of the other. He whipped the knife from the first man and plunged it into the chest of the second. The man gasped. His eyes looked up at Harvey, big and white, pleading, understanding. Harvey twisted the blade and jerked it out, letting the man fall to the ground.

Shouts began to come from the cabin, not Adeo's but foreign. An older man's voice. Luan.

Harvey strode along the sidewall of the property. Two men crept around the corner in front of him. One looked behind as the other breached the corner, using tactical manoeuvres. These two were military trained, not like the others he had come across. Harvey raised his Sig and took them both down with two shots. The shots seemed to wake the dead. Shouts rang out from all directions across the yard, and scattered footsteps approached from all directions. Harvey turned one more corner, looking for a place to duck into and gather his thoughts. He turned and stepped into the muzzle of a waiting AK-74.

---

Harvey stared down the barrel into the man's eyes. He was calm, not breathing heavily, and wasn't excited. It wasn't his first time; he was a pro and would probably be ready for an attack from Harvey. Harvey dropped his Sig to the ground and raised his empty hands.

"Walk," said the man.

Harvey didn't move.

"I told you to walk, so walk."

"Where am I walking?" Harvey was waiting for the footsteps of more men, joining the man to celebrate their capture, but none did. He was alone, which told Harvey that the only other men were in the cabin.

"Just fucking walk or I'll drop you right here."

A three round burst from Melody's barking dog turned the man's cold expression into shock, horror and pain. He twisted and dropped to his knees. Harvey picked up his Sig and put the gun to the man's head. He looked up at Melody and pulled the trigger.

"What took you so long?"

"Ah well, you know, traffic, the weather," said Melody. "I'm glad you're okay. Let's get out of here before-"

She was cut off by the noise of two engines starting. They ducked into the line of cars and watched as the BMW and Range Rover sped out the gates and into the night.

"Reg, come back," said Melody into her earpiece.

"Go ahead."

Two vehicles just left the yard. Can you track them? BMW and a black Range Rover."

"Yeah, I see the Range Rover. I have his plate. Let me see what I can do."

Melody turned back to Harvey. "Are you coming with us?"

"Wait in the van. I need to check the cabin."

Melody looked through the cars to the cabin. It was shielded by piles of scrap. "You think he's still in there?"

"Adeo? Probably not. But we might find something else in there."

"I can't read you, Harvey."

"Don't try then."

"Are you going to save Adeo or kill him yourself?" She handed Harvey a fresh clip for his Sig, knowing that he would be running low.

"To be honest, Melody," he said, sliding the new magazine into place, "I haven't decided yet."

"It would be nice to get some arrests at the end of this, not just a pile of bodies." Melody gestured at the yard, which had men lying on cars, feet and legs sticking out from between piles of junk and one flamethrower with its docile flame tapering off into the air.

"He knows too much. I can't risk him talking. Wait in the van. I'll be out in a sec."

"No, Harvey. I'm coming with you. I've already missed most of the action. At least let me search the cabin with you."

Harvey sighed. "Okay, let's move. In and out. One minute."

The pair ran to the door of the cabin. The lights were on, but there was no movement inside. Melody stood to one side of the door, her MP5 held ready to fire. Harvey kicked the door in, sending it across the floor inside. Melody was in and aiming her weapon at all the blind corners. Harvey stepped in behind her. There were two rooms, both of equal size, approximately four metres wide by six metres. The first was a mess room with a long central table and chairs, presumably where the men would sit and drink coffee and smoke. Two large filing cabinets stood to one side containing scrap records and logbooks of some of the cars that passed through, probably the bare minimum to keep the taxman and law at bay. There were calendars of topless women on the walls, and overflowing ashtrays on the tables, plus empty Vodka bottles dotted around like ornaments.

The second room was Luan's office. A large, glossy desk stood in front of a cushioned, leather reclining chair. There were two less comfortable chairs on the guest side and a potted plant in the corner.

There was no paperwork in the desk drawers, no photos on top, and no sign of anybody being in there, only the smell of cigarette smoke and the musky scent of old sweat.

"Jackson, be ready to go in two," said Melody into her comms.

"Copy," came the reply.

"Dead end," said Melody. "Let's hope Reg managed to get a track on the Range Rover."

"This isn't his main office. This is just a convenient spot for him to work when he's in the area. He's got a main office somewhere else, somewhere slightly more welcoming," said Harvey.

"I'd also say he's got somewhere *less* welcoming for Adeo, and that's where they're heading."

"I'd agree with that," said Harvey. "Let's move."

"Wait," said Melody, then she lost her momentum and added weakly, "are you going to tell me about it?"

"About what, Melody?"

"You saw your foster father, after all this time. I thought, well-"

"There's nothing to think about. He's a villain, I'm not. I've paid my dues."

"You think he'll blow your cover?"

"If I go back without Adeo, maybe. Otherwise, I'm doing him a favour. I just need to make sure I corner him, have a chat, get a lay of the land. I'm sure he'll realise that I'd be slaughtered if he lets on that my name is not Gerry and I've been lying to the firm. I can't imagine he'd want that to happen. But he didn't get where he is by being nice, did he?"

"Let's move," said Melody, and turned to the door. She stepped down the three small steps as Harvey followed then heard the familiar sound of an AK being cocked.

"Drop your weapons," said the man.

Harvey gave a long slow whistle. "You're good," he said.

"No games. Drop them."

Harvey heard the sound he was waiting for, the scatter of mud and light rhythm of dogs' feet bounding across the yard. Movement caught the man's eye, and he turned to see two airborne fifty-pound German Shepherds with bared teeth.

The dogs took him down with no effort and tore through his throat with the savage, carnal ferocity of wolves.

Harvey nudged Melody as she stood and looked on in horror.

"Let's move."

## 12

## BALL AND CHAIN

"Talk to me, Ginger," said John Cartwright. He was sat alone at a table for two in an Italian restaurant on the Isle of Dogs. The waiter had just delivered his lobster linguine. He sipped at an expensive glass of Chianti and waited for his new number two to deliver the update.

"It's Adeo, boss. Gerry just walked out with some bird. No sign of Adeo."

"Talk me through it."

"Well, they were in there about half an hour when the place erupted. Sounded like a bloody movie. Two cars came tearing out and the bird walked in carrying a machine gun. I haven't got a clue where she came from. Then there was a few more shots, and the pair of them walked out like they just had dinner."

"Did anybody follow the cars?"

"No, boss, we're on our own here. We expected to see Adeo and that Gerry bloke come running out any minute."

"You think Adeo is down?"

"I just poked my head in the gates and saw two massive dogs. Nothing else moving. He's either dead or in the car."

"Well, if we lose Adeo, I want Bobby and his firm taken care of and dumped in the river, Ginger."

"Sorry, boss."

"Don't apologise to me, Ging. But make plans. Make sure we're ready to jump the lot of them as soon as I give the word."

"Will do, boss."

"What about the bird? Who is she?"

"Dunno, boss. She looks serious. She's got filth written all over her."

"A cop?"

"Who else has automatic weapons like that? Besides, it's the way she held it, like she'd trained, you know what I mean?"

"Are you following them?"

"Yeah, they just walked up the road. I'll find out where they're going and get back to you."

"Make sure you do, Ginger."

---

"This is more like it," said Reg as the van pulled away. "The whole team back in the van, just like the old days."

Melody didn't reply. The statement reminded her that Denver wasn't there.

"How are you getting on with finding that Range Rover, Reg?" asked Harvey.

"Done. Easy. LUCY is tracking it now. I just traced the plates back to the dealer, hacked the dealer's firewall and-"

"Another time, eh Reg? Sorry mate, it's been a rough night."

"Reg, where am I heading?" asked Jackson.

"A12, Jackson, all the way," replied Reg. "Looks like

they've stopped in some kind of recycling plant off Pudding Mill Lane."

"Mark the exits for me, Reg. I'll take a look in a minute. Jackson, can you call out the ETAs? Melody, how many spare clips you got for the Sigs?"

"Two each."

"So, four for me then. You're staying in the van."

"No, I'm not. I just sat outside and listened to world war three going off in that yard."

"You'll blow my cover. I need to go in and get Adeo and get out. If I have help, he'll know I'm still old bill. At least if I work alone, I may be able to convince him otherwise."

"For god's sake, Harvey."

"Sorry to interrupt, people, but we have a tail," said Jackson. "They've been on us since we left the yard."

Harvey was sat on the floor of the van behind Melody in the passenger seat. "Melody, how close?"

"Two hundred metres give or take."

"Reckon you can make the shot?"

"What? Harvey, we're not on a random killing rampage."

"No, we're running an operation to stop organised crime. Can you make the shot or not?"

"No, Harvey, I won't do it."

Harvey pulled his Sig from his waistband. "Jackson, take us somewhere quiet."

"What are you doing, Harvey?" said Melody.

"Stopping organised crime, Melody. What does it look like I'm doing?"

"I know a place around the corner. We'll be there in one minute," said Jackson.

"Reg, on my three."

"No," said Melody. "Stop, everyone. Just stop."

"No time, Melody. We're in this now," said Harvey.

"Thirty seconds," said Jackson.

"Reg, be ready with the door."

"Harvey, what are you doing?"

"Melody, do you trust me?"

"With my life. But this is stupid."

"Ten seconds."

"Get that barking dog of yours, and be ready to jump out on my one." He'd turned and spoken the words carefully at her, looking her directly in the eye.

Melody made the MP5 ready and sat with her hand on the door handle. "Frank isn't going to like this."

Harvey felt the van turn right. Trees hung across the road, and only old warehouses stood either side.

"Three."

Jackson eased off the accelerator pedal, and the van began to slow. The car behind drew close.

"Two." Reg pulled the handle on the rear door and shoved it open as hard as he could.

Harvey fired twice at the car's radiator, and angry steam hissed from the grill.

"One."

Melody dived out of the passenger seat and covered the car with the MP5.

Harvey began to slide out the van. "Tyres."

Melody gave two three-round bursts and took out the front and back right tires.

Harvey strode to the driver's door and ripped it open with his weapon on the driver. He reached in and dragged the man to the tarmac. Harvey stood on the back of his neck and aimed at the passenger. "It's Ginger, right? The man with the head in the bag?"

The man nodded.

"You've got three seconds to get out the car before I finish you right here. Try anything dumb, and she'll open you up. One."

The man opened the door.

"Two."

He slowly stepped out with his hands raised.

"Three. Good. When I give you an order with a time limit, do it faster. Next time, I won't be so lenient." Harvey's eyes never left the man who stood close to Melody. "Reg, ties."

Reg grabbed a bundle of zip ties and climbed out the van. He passed them to Harvey.

"I don't want them, zip this up," said Harvey. He had full control of the situation. "Put two or three on, they're going in the back with you." Once Reg had pulled the man's hands behind his back and had the first tie pulled tight, Harvey released pressure off his neck and walked round to Ginger.

"You're considering running."

"No, I'm not, honest I-"

"Yeah, you are. I saw you looking about."

"I didn't, I weren't-"

Harvey fired a round into the man's foot. "No running."

The man fell to the ground with an inaudible whimper.

"Reg, tie this one up." Harvey walked back to the driver. "Up." The man struggled to roll over with bound hands, so Harvey leaned down, grabbed his collar and gave him a yank to help him stand. "In the back."

Once Ginger had been loaded up, Melody climbed into the passenger seat, and Harvey sat on top of the two men. He pulled the door closed. "Gerry says go," said Harvey, reminding the team not to use his real name. "ETA?" he called.

"Less than five minutes out."

He tapped Reg on the shoulder. "Show me the exits, mate," said Harvey, keeping the use of names out of the conversation. "And good work back there, nice and quick."

Reg turned smiling, and said, "Thanks, Ha-"

"Exits," said Harvey, warning Reg not to use his name.

"Here we are," said Reg, diverting his sentence. "One main gate at the front, a smaller gate at the side in a quiet street, and nothing at the back except a high wall and the canal. The satellite is live, so I've scrolled back a few hours and found this daylight shot from earlier."

Harvey memorised the layout of the site. It looked to be fairly large, maybe a few acres, with a group of three buildings in one corner. There were heaps of scrap metal, white goods and piles of randomly assorted recycling shown on the satellite imagery.

"Okay, driver, side entrance please."

"I'm coming with you," said Melody.

Harvey didn't reply.

"You hear me, Gerry?"

Harvey was tightening his laces. "You're taking these two in."

"You can't go alone, Gerry."

"One minute," said Jackson.

"Track me, follow me, do what you need to do. I'll let you know if I need help."

"And how do you plan on doing that?"

Harvey nudged Reg again. "Got an earpiece?"

Reg passed Harvey an earpiece from a small bag on his bench. Harvey removed the hygiene wrapper and slotted it into his ear. He hit the tiny button twice for the channel to stay open without the need for the push-to-talk. "Take these guys in. Come back for me," said Harvey, looking Melody in the eye to reassure her without embarrassing her. "Driver, what's the ETA on HQ and back?"

"Forty minutes, including drop off time."

"I'll be out in thirty-five. If I'm not, come looking for me."

"Ten seconds," said Jackson.

Harvey banged his Sig lightly on the head of one of the men beneath him. "While I'm gone, I'd like one of you to do me a favour." He spoke slowly and clearly. "I want you to tell these nice people where I can find John Cartwright." One of the men struggled as the van came to a stop. Harvey nodded for Reg to open the rear door. "Because I promise you, if you wait for me to get back and I have to ask you, it's going to hurt a lot more, and for a lot longer. Is that understood?"

No reply.

Harvey bent down between the men's heads and offered a growling whisper. "I said, is that understood?"

The men waited for a few seconds then both nodded.

Harvey stepped off the back of the van and reached up to close the door. He caught Melody turning in her seat, watching him with worry in her eyes.

He winked and closed the door, then turned and stepped into the waiting open gate.

---

Reg opened the sliding shutter doors of the team's headquarters using LUCY's console. Jackson pulled the van in and the shutters slid back in place.

Melody opened the van's sliding side door and spoke to the two men. "Out."

"What are we going to do with them?" asked Reg.

"Find me some handcuffs, Reg," replied Melody. "Come on, you two. Out."

The two villains slid backwards out the van and stood.

"Where are we?" asked Ginger.

"No questions, just move. See that column over there?"

A steel girder supported the mezzanine floor. It was bolted top and bottom.

"I'm sure you know the drill. Stand with your backs to the beam," ordered Melody.

Reg returned with two sets of handcuffs from Melody's filing cabinet. Melody raised the MP5 to her shoulder and aimed at the two men. "Okay, cut the ties, and cuff them back to back around the column."

"No problem, I've been tying people up all night," said Reg.

"Driver?" called Melody. "Can you cover these two while I get some ammo?"

Jackson walked over to Melody, took the MP5, and placed the butt into Ginger's shoulder.

"You've fired one of these before. That looks natural."

"I've been known to help out here and there," said Jackson with a smile.

"Good to know. Make sure those cuffs are tight and uncomfortable."

The team were ready in under five minutes.

"Okay, you two, Ginger, wasn't it? And what's your name?" The man didn't reply.

"You want to tell me where we can find John Cartwright?"

"Not really, miss," said Ginger.

"It'd work in your favour if you did."

"Is that right? I'd have my throat slit, and even if I went away, he'd get me on the inside. I'm not telling you nothing."

"Well, I'll tell you right now, this is the easy option. If you talk, I can get you in witness protection. Nobody can find you."

"Yeah right, you don't know John Cartwright."

"Oh, believe me, we know John Cartwright better than anyone."

"No, save your breath, lady. You've got twenty-four hours to charge me, and I want my legal rep if you do."

Melody laughed. "Honestly, look at us. You really think

that conventional rules apply here? You two aren't who we're after. You're small fry, not worth the paperwork. The number of men Gerry put down tonight, two more wouldn't make a difference. So your options are simple. Talk to me, or *Gerry* will make you talk."

"You talk like he's some sort of legend. Who is he? Ex-SAS or something?"

Melody laughed again. "No, but you're right, he is a legend." Melody stood and turned to walk away. "But I'll tell you this, Ginger."

Ginger looked up at Melody. "What? Tell me what? He's going to pull my fingernails out?"

"Fingernails? No." She walked back to him and looked him in the eye. "If you don't tell Gerry where we can find Cartwright, he won't stop at you. He'll find your family."

"Behave. He wouldn't be allowed, he-"

"Who do you think he is, you idiot? He's not police, he's one of you. He's a villain, a lifelong villain. He's been killing people since he was twelve years old, and he's pretty good at it. Piss him off, go on, I dare you. I guarantee he'll bring your wife here and let you watch him."

"You're talking out of your arse, bitch. No cops can do that."

Melody laughed. "We're not cops. We don't exist. Look at where you are. Not very nick-like is it? Wake up, Ginger. You're in for a rough ride, and your ticket to surviving is slipping away."

Melody turned to Reg. "Can you stay here and keep an eye on these two? Any problems, use your weapon."

"Me? But I-"

"Keep calm. They can't go anywhere, but better safe than sorry. Besides, we need you on LUCY."

Reg looked slightly dejected. "Okay, I guess."

"Driver, we ready to go?"

"Let's do it."

Melody spoke softly into the comms. "Gerry, no need to reply, but our ETA is..." She looked at Jackson who mimed fifteen minutes. "Fifteen minutes. That's one-five minutes. Click three times if you need something."

Jackson put the van into reverse and pulled out the unit. Ginger's eyes met Melody's as she disappeared from view.

"That was impressive," said Jackson. "Powerful."

"That was desperate, Jackson."

Jackson put the van into first and pulled away as the sliding shutters closed. "How do you mean?"

"If they *don't* talk to Harvey, he'll rip them to shreds. I was *trying* to save their lives."

## 13

# RED HERRING

HARVEY SURVEYED THE DARK RECYCLING PLANT IN FRONT of him. The satellite image he'd seen on Reg's screen mapped the scene out for him. The three buildings were in the far right-hand corner, and there was no sign of movement. Harvey took a path around the edge of the plot alongside the high wall, keeping to the shadows and moving slow, always listening and watching. It was during these times that Harvey's mind was most alive, like a Neolithic man walking through the African bush, always alert for dangers, always having an escape route, and most of all, always having a plan.

The few times he had to cross open land, he encountered no trouble. The lack of security told him two things. Firstly, Duri was not expecting to be followed or tracked, and secondly, the site had limited men. The scrapyard had been full of men. He and Adeo had taken a lot of them down. Now Harvey just needed a plan to tear his way through the rest of them.

He came upon the buildings. They were laid out in a large L-shape, with the third building far longer than the rest. Harvey supposed this to be the offices. The other two structures were smaller, ten metres by twenty, Harvey thought. He stood between the outer wall of the compound and the first small building. It smelled damp, and the windows were opaque with wire mesh. Harvey took a guess that this was the toilet and shower block. The next building had lights on in one of the rooms. Harvey stepped slowly up to see in, but the room was empty. It was a small office for a two people. Two old telephones stood on two old desks, with two battered old chairs behind them.

There were no nude calendars, no empty bottles of vodka and no overspilling ashtrays. He felt around the window. It was locked. The area was fairly rough, so security would be quite high. Yet the gate had been left open, possibly because of the speed at which they were travelling, and possibly because they weren't planning on staying long.

He heard footsteps on the boarded floor inside. Heavy boots. A door slammed shut somewhere, and men's voices vibrated through the thin walls, but Harvey couldn't understand the language.

At least two, Duri and one other.

Then Harvey heard voices from outside. Two more. The tone of the first on the inside suggested hierarchy. One was sharper and shorter, the other more appeasing. The two voices around the corner sounded more conversational, equals.

Harvey chanced a glance around the corner. Two men stood smoking. An AK-74 leaned against the wall behind one of them. The other had one hand in his pocket. They were relaxed, confident that nobody would come. One of the two men took a casual look around him. Harvey ducked his head back and heard the men walk away. He watched them disappear into the middle of the yard, then turn behind a pile of white goods.

Harvey followed.

He stepped quietly onto patches of dry mud, around puddles and through muddy tyre tracks. It was pitch dark in the yard, and Harvey could hear nothing.

Until the lights came on.

Two powerful spotlights atop an earthmoving machine forty metres in front of him lit the ground where Harvey stood, followed by the roar of its powerful diesel engine starting up. Harvey froze. He was in plain sight. Another pair of spotlights lit him from behind, and another diesel engine began to cough into life. As if in sync, lights came from either side of him. The air was filled now with the spitting and deep throaty growl of four engines. He had nowhere to run.

The un-oiled squealing of the machine's heavy iron tracks joined the ensemble, and the bass-like rumble of thirty tons of heavy machinery filled the lower spectrum of sound. Hanging chains from the heavy steel bulldozers rattled in percussive shudders as the enormous machines slowly closed in on Harvey.

The ground was now well lit and Harvey saw the silhouettes of many men filling the gaps between each machine. Each perfect human shape was scarred with the unmistakable barrel of a Kalashnikov.

Harvey growled at his own stupidity under his breath. Patience, planning and execution, his mantra. He'd acted hastily to save his own life. But by doing so, he now saw no other option than to lay down his weapon.

He held fast as long as he could until the machines were each just ten metres away. He was boxed in by the steel, diesel-powered monsters, and the grit and tenacity of the Albanian mafia.

The engines were cut, and the silence that followed the deathly chorus seemed to linger as if in appreciation.

"You are a brave man," said a voice, the old man's voice, Duri.

Harvey didn't reply.

"Stupid, but brave." The man in the long coat stepped out of the glare of lights and towards Harvey, but stopped three metres in front of him. "Did you really think that just two men could destroy us? Do you see what we have built here in your country?"

"All I see is a bunch of immigrants on a piece of land that nobody else wants."

"Ah, we see things with different eyes though, do we not?" The man began to walk in a circle around Harvey. Harvey stayed perfectly still, all too aware of the twenty AK-74s that were aimed at him.

"You see, where you see wasteland, I see opportunity. Where you see the unwanted items of the rich, I see profit for the poor people of Albania, my homeland." He spoke the last two words softly, with affection.

"I don't care about the waste, have it. But you over-stepped the mark, didn't you? You couldn't help yourself, right? You just wanted one more piece of the pie. Well, that pie belongs to us. London? We might let you live here, and yeah, we let you send your money home. That's just humanity. But each time you stand on someone else's toes, you disrupt a very delicate balance."

"How poetic. You like poetry?"

"Not particularly."

"It's shame. Poetry is a beautiful way to capture our history. So many great poems describe times long ago that we strive to understand today. In fact, poetry is the only record of certain historical events and is the basis of our knowledge. Like a verbal tapestry."

"Please tell me I'm not standing here in the mud talking about poetry with a pikey? Is this how it ends? I thought I'd have a more peaceful death if I'm honest."

"Tell me what they'd write about you. The poets."

Harvey didn't reply.

"Tell me who you are."

Harvey didn't reply.

"You'll talk, of that I'm sure. I have skills. I was taught by the best."

"We share an enthusiasm for encouragement. Aleksander spoke too. I was amazed at how quickly he spoke if I'm honest. A big bloke like that reduced to tears and pissing himself."

Luan glared at Harvey.

"Tell me who you are."

"I'm going to need a little more encouragement than that, Luan."

"You want encouragement?"

"Do it."

"You want to piss your pants like Aleksander?"

"Make me. Let's play."

"You're a crazy fool."

"Yeah, maybe. But let me make one thing clear, when the tables turn, and it's you who needs encouragement, I'm going to make you sing. Bear that in mind, and we'll see who sings loudest, eh?"

Luan laughed. "Such control." He stopped laughing, took on a serious grimace and stared into Harvey's eyes. "I look forward to breaking you." He nodded to the man behind Harvey.

Harvey felt the butt of a rifle slam into the back of his head. Blood rushed to his brain, he tasted iron, and darkness enveloped him.

---

Harvey woke stripped naked in a windowless room with rough concrete walls. His wrists were bound with a harsh manila rope, which was fixed to chains that hung from a steel eye bolt in the concrete ceiling above. A single lamp to his right barely lit the ten-foot-square room, and a single chair sat opposite him where Luan Duri sat calmly, staring at Harvey.

"Good morning," said Luan.

Harvey's head throbbed, and his back was aching like he'd been dragged across the concrete floor.

"Did you sleep well?"

It was pointless to try to work out where in the compound he was. If he was actually still in the compound. His watch had been removed; he had no idea how long he'd been out for. All Harvey could do was prepare himself for what was to come. To survive.

"You interest me," said Luan. "I do so wish to know your name. It would make the conversation so much more engaging if I knew who I'm talking to."

Harvey didn't reply.

"You'll tell me. Eventually."

Luan stood and walked around the back of Harvey.

"So, perhaps we can start with something easy. We do, after all, have all night. Longer if need be." Luan leaned over Harvey's shoulder and spoke quietly into his left ear. "Tell me about Aleksander, our mutual friend. Tell me how you made him talk."

Harvey didn't reply. He felt something cold and hard trace the muscles on his back.

"You take good care of yourself."

Harvey felt the point of a blade in the small of his back.

"Tell me," whispered Luan.

"I didn't touch him," spat Harvey.

"Oh, come on. The silence I can deal with, but lies, I cannot tolerate liars."

"He spoke freely against you."

"Did you...encourage him?"

"I didn't need to."

The blade slid up Harvey's spine and stopped between his shoulder blades. "One of the things I enjoy about what you call encouragement is the exploratory elements. I regard it as a lesson in science. For example, I once opened a man and removed various parts of him. I did it slowly, of course, such matters require delicacy, or else the heart will fail and spoil my fun."

He leaned over Harvey's right shoulder and whispered. "Shall we have a science lesson?" He stopped. "Do you notice you are missing some items?"

It was then that Harvey realised the earpiece had gone. The blade ran further up Harvey's back until it found the wound where the tracker that Melody had inserted had been. It had been removed.

"You see now why you interest me?" said Luan. "More so than the giant in the next room, your friend."

Luan stepped in front of Harvey. "Do you want to know what I think?"

"Not really."

"I think you're with an agency. SO10 maybe? SOCA?"

Harvey didn't reply.

"I have been in Britain long enough to know that even SO10 are not permitted to kill without approval. Yet you, my friend, well you created quite a body count in my yard, didn't you? I'll admit that they were not perhaps my best men, good men are hard to come by, but you made it all look so effortless."

Luan paced around Harvey once more.

"If you're holding out for rescue, then I am afraid I have bad news for you. Everything you owned, your clothes, your phone, your little devices, are all on a journey a long way from here. So you may be here some time."

Luan stepped close to Harvey and looked deep into his eyes. Then Harvey felt Luan's hand on his genitals. "How about our science lesson? I'm done talking. Now it is your turn." Luan squeezed hard. Harvey bit down on his lip and breathed out hard through his nose.

Luan released his grip. "Impressive. You're a real man's man, aren't you?"

Harvey didn't reply.

"I think I'll start with something smaller," said Luan. "I'll save the best for last." Luan licked his lips slowly. "An ear maybe? Or a toe? What do you think?"

"I think you're writing a cheque you can't afford, pal."

"Is that so?" Luan looked thoughtfully around the room then stepped into the shadows. Harvey heard the clatter of tools on a bench. Then Luan stepped back into the light holding an axe handle.

"Did you miss me?" said Luan, and then swung the bat.

———

"Fast as you can, Jackson. I don't want to miss the party," said Melody. Jackson opened up the throttle on the VW van.

"Reg, talk to me. How's he looking?"

"Well, he's on the move."

"He's moving? Where?"

"In transit, now. His phone, tracker and earpiece are all moving east."

"What's he doing? Can we get him on the comms?"

"Without the antenna on the van, the earpiece relies on GPS or satellite. Looking at the keep-alive report, he went dark ten minutes ago, and is now heading east at fifty miles an hour."

"Be my eyes, Reg," said Jackson. "Where am I going?"

Melody was taken back by the phrase 'be my eyes.'

Denver used to say that in times just like the one they found themselves in.

"Head to the North Circular Road. You can cut in or out of town from there. I'll keep you posted."

"We're screwed if we lose him, Jackson."

"Then we better not lose him." Jackson looked across at Melody. She was a tough girl, but she clearly had feelings for Harvey. They'd shared so many adventures already that somehow she loved him. Jackson was good at reading people. He was intuitive to people's feelings.

"Reg, it's Jackson."

"Go ahead."

"Put me through to a Chief Superintendent Fox with the Hackney Police."

"What are you doing?" asked Melody. "This is covert. We can't call it in. Do you know what we did back there?"

"Trust me, Melody. Fox owes me."

"I'm working on it. It's out of hours, so I'll need to find his mobile, and they like to hide those. Fortunately, I like to find them, and...here it is. Sit tight caller."

The comms was routed to the phone call and the van's loudspeaker.

"Fox." The voice answered abruptly.

"CS Fox, it's Jackson."

There was a long silence. "I wondered when you'd call it in."

"I wouldn't if I had a choice, sir."

"I hear you're on the dark side now?"

"Dark in terms of viability, but always on the side of the law."

"Okay, what is it? And why?"

"A bird, sir. I'm afraid I can't tell you any more than that."

"I can't just release a chopper without good reason, Jackson. You know that."

"I thought we had a deal, sir."

"We did have a deal."

"And you owe me."

"I do owe you, but I was expecting maybe you'd use that to release a friend who was caught drink driving or something."

"I'd never ask you to do that, sir. You know my view on DD."

"But you can second a police helicopter without good reason? Where are you taking it?"

"Sir, do you trust me?"

"I used to."

"It's covert, sir. If I could tell you, I would, I'd even call you in to help. There's enough glory in this one to hang a few medals off your tunic."

Fox gave a heavy sigh. "I suppose you want me to clear the bird with ATC too?"

"It'd save a lot of embarrassing questions, sir."

"Give me five minutes. Call me back."

---

"Dom, tell me where we're at."

"Bobby, they're cleaned out. Our men are inside now. We've hit every bookie they protect, and we've got men outside all the pubs."

"Any resistance from the owners?"

"One or two. Most turned around easy, happy to be looked after by natives, as it were."

"Good, good. I want twenty good men in the area, I want to be seen, and I want the locals to know that Bobby Carnell now runs the manor, and they no longer need to fear the Albanians."

"You reckon John Cartwright will strike?"

"No, Dom, I don't. Right now John Cartwright is probably sitting feeding his greedy face, more concerned with what Gerry and his goon are doing. Leave Doug here with me. He can run things while you're expanding the business. Once the Albanians are out of the way, Dom, I'll sort you out, mate. You've done well."

"Cheers, Bobby."

"Remember, any sign of an Albanian in the area, and you take them out. From what Sid said, Gerry and Adeo created an absolute bloodbath, said it was like a scene from a film. Pretty soon, they won't have the men to do anything about it, and they'll have to go elsewhere. Home hopefully. Make some friends, Dom, buy some drinks, work out what local boys we have there, get them on board. You know how it works. Don't say too much, but work out where the extra hands are if we need them."

"Will do, Bobby. But listen, mate, I've been thinking. This John Cartwright, he's old school, right?"

"Yeah. So?"

"So how many times has someone like Cartwright walked brazenly into another firm's boozer, stared the main man in the eye and pretty much forced him to do something, like take on another firm."

Bobby was silent.

"You see what I mean, Bobby? I reckon once the Albanians are gone, he'll come after us."

"Behave. He's not looking for a war between us. He keeps to his turf we keep to ours. Respect, Dom, that's what it's all about."

"Yeah, but we're not keeping to our own, are we? Here I am on the border of North London, making sure the Albanians don't come back. It's going to piss him off, Bobby."

"So, we take John Cartwright out. I am not backing down, Dom. Don't get weak."

"I'm not getting weak. You know me, Bobby. I'm just sitting here piecing it all together."

"Right, well while you're sitting there, piece together a plan so we can off Cartwright. I'll get some boys in East Ham to have a look at where he's dug in."

"What about Gerry, Bobby? I don't trust him."

"Gerry who, Dom?"

# 14

## DAWN OF DEATH

HARVEY FOUGHT FOR BREATH. LUAN HAD JUST FINISHED another round of wild swings on his back, and his lungs had taken a beating. He could taste blood. His legs had given way from the repeated strikes to his balls, which were now swollen and angry red. He hung from the chains and revelled in the break.

"Pretty soon I will move to something a little sharper," said Luan. "Are you sure you wouldn't like to tell me your name?"

*My name,* thought Harvey. *What the hell is my name? Am I Gerry now? Harvey Stone wouldn't be here. He was smarter than that.*

"I'm talking to you," said Luan.

*Gerry may have gotten me into this mess, but it'll be Harvey who gets me out.*

"Bardh," called Luan.

The door opened after a few seconds. A man with a shaved head and tattoos on his face opened the door.

"Boss?" said Bardh in a deep grumble. He wasn't a particularly big man, not compared to Adeo or Julios, but he looked fit and strong. His skin hugged his unshaved face, and his dark features were prominent in the dim light.

"Bring me the goon, Bardh."

The door closed.

"You're going to enjoy this," said Luan.

"Am I? I can't say I'm thrilled right now."

"Well, I'm going to enjoy it anyway."

The door opened again, and four men brought Adeo inside. Two held Kalashnikov assault rifles, while the other two manhandled him into the room. Someone brought steps in and fixed chains to the eye bolt in the ceiling beside Harvey.

"Now leave me," said Luan. "Go find some food. I can watch them. Bring me something."

The door closed, and Luan sat on the single wooden chair in front of Harvey and Adeo. He reached into the inside pocket of his long coat and pulled out a fillet knife. He held the weapon easily, as if he was accustomed to handling that particular knife. Luan flexed it and studied the edge for nicks and small chips on the finest part of a blade, but there were none.

"When I was a boy, my father taught me to fish," said Luan. The statement wasn't particularly aimed at either one of the two men that hung from the ceiling like carcasses of game. It was an opening line for his story, and he spoke like John Cartwright had spoken of Harvey's parents. Like it was rehearsed. A speech. Verbatim.

"We had a small house in a small village with a river that carved its way through the fields like snake. My mother was always at home, always something to do, cleaning and cooking or sewing. She made our clothes, you know. We had chickens for eggs, and we grew vegetables, potatoes and such. Money was tight and food was expensive. The horror of the war still hung in the air, and people clung to memories of lost children, parents, family. It was a dark time in a bitter cold winter. Nobody looked to the future, the present was hard to ignore. But my father was a strong man. He taught me to hunt and to fish, so often we would sit in a small rowboat on one of the many lakes, and we would sit and talk and catch fish. We never caught too many, only enough to feed us and occasionally we would catch one for our neighbour. To trade. My father never spoke of the war. I always imagined it was because the horrors were too much for a child to learn of. But since, I have learned that it was he who performed the horrors, and so I surmised that he had been ashamed of his acts. I wonder if he could see me now, if he could see how I understand. Maybe he would have told me those things he did. Maybe he would have taught me. Father and son, sharing a kill. There's something poetic about that, isn't there?"

He looked at Harvey who had been studying his face as he told the story.

"I told you, poetry runs through our very existence. I'm sorry, Adeo, I was referring to a conversation that we had before you arrived. How rude of me."

Luan dropped his head again and continued with his story. "My father did teach me how to use a knife. This very knife in fact. It was his own, and then he passed it to me. A man bonds with his knife, doesn't he? There's something special about a well-crafted knife that surpasses any connection a man may have with a gun or a rifle. My father showed me how to gut a fish. Then he showed me how to clean it by opening it up. When I was expert at both, he showed me how to use my knife to cut the fillet from the bone. At first, I found bones in my food, sharp reminders that my lessons were not over. But after some time, I was practised and moved on to chickens, and then bigger and tougher animals."

Luan looked up at Harvey who stared back.

"Am I boring you?"

Harvey didn't reply.

"There was a family in our village, rough people, and dirty. They stole from the villagers, and the father went to prison. Soon the family became so poor the mother could barely feed her children. I found her eldest son in our house one day. My mother was feeding the chickens and my father was out somewhere working the fields with other villagers. The boy was older than me by a year, maybe two. I stepped into the kitchen, and he turned to face me, unafraid but ashamed. His pockets were full of the fruit my mother had picked, and the bread she had baked. The boy turned to walk away, and I let him. I watched him leave, and he looked back at me as he closed the door of our house. I followed that boy through the windows as he walked around the side, and then to the front, where he disappeared into the narrow lane that led to their house. I checked my mother was not around then I slipped out of the house after him. His shame had been forgotten in our kitchen. He walked along eating our fruit, skipping puddles of rain. He looked like boy who hadn't care in the world. No father had ever taught that boy to fish, and gather food for his family. No father had ever showed that boy that life can be bearable with a little hard work, that obstacles are there to face on your own, and that stealing from another is not the answer."

Luan paused and looked back up. "That was my first time. My first kill." Luan held the blade lovingly. "I took all those lessons my father taught me and went to work. I fought the boy and knocked him down with a rock. I dragged the boy into the thick bushes that lined the sparse fields. I cut him open like a carp, and I removed his insides. I filleted the boy, and I ate his liver."

There was a long silence before Harvey spoke.

"How did it taste?" He felt Adeo's eyes on him and caught

the cold snarly smile of Luan Duri. Just the corners of his mouth upturned.

"Delicious," said Luan. "Like the first meat I ever really tasted."

"And you ate more?"

"They were desperate times. Food could not be wasted."

"And they were hard times too, wasn't they? A killer could not be caught or he would surely pay the ultimate price."

"You listen well," said Luan. "Can I ask, have you tried it? Human flesh?"

Harvey didn't reply.

"You were doing so well. But you may be pleased to know that my little anecdote is now over. It is now your turn to entertain me with your own stories. I am sure that you both have many, so I will do a deal with you." Luan rose and dragged the chair into the corner of the room. Then he walked behind the two naked men. "Each of you will tell me one story, something horrific. *I* will judge. *I* will decide who dies first. But this I will not tell you. I will not tell you what I am looking for. Am I looking for gruesome? Or am I looking to see who has the strongest morality? I may be looking for a story to tell my grandchildren or I may be looking to see who deserves to die first. But I will tell you this, the winner will die fast and relatively painlessly. The other, well, not so fast and not so painlessly. Is that understood?"

Adeo nodded. Harvey just stared at the floor.

"Begin."

Harvey lifted his head and sensed Luan close behind him, urging him to talk.

"I had a sister once," began Harvey, "when I was young. She died." Harvey closed his eyes and dragged the memories he'd fought so hard to bury back to the front of his mind. "Some bad men took her and..." He swallowed hard through his parched throat. "She was just a child, barely fifteen. I was twelve at the time, and I'll never forget the night it happened. I heard her screams, and I heard their breath destroying her with each stroke. I sat in the shadows and listened, helpless. She killed herself a few days later. She stole a knife from the kitchen and took it to her room, where she stabbed herself in all the places they had touched. Squeezed. Penetrated."

"This is good," said Luan. "Do go on."

"I found the first man six months later, and with the help of a friend, I took him down. I made him suffer. Eventually, I killed him. I felt a small amount of peace for Hannah. But I hadn't finished. It took me twenty years, but I found the next man. He'd been close all along. I'd seen him every day, and every day as I grew stronger, and the twelve-year-old boy grew into a man, he feared that the day would come when I found out his dirty secret and would bring more peace to Hannah."

Harvey took a moment to push the memory of Jack aside, and bring forward the memory of Sergio. "Sergio was a coward. A numbers man with long bony fingers that were in every little nook and crack. He knew everything and controlled everything with his knowledge. I boiled Sergio alive in an antique copper bathtub. I watched his eyes turn pale white, blinded as the liquids inside them boiled. I watched as, one by one, his organs failed. Cooked. Ready to eat."

"Like a boil in the bag?" Luan smiled.

"Like a boil in the bag, Luan. As he died, he gave me the name the last man who had been there, the last man who'd raped my sister. Again, I hunted and found him. I took him to the very same place where I had boiled his friend alive. He was a villain, a cold-hearted villain with little sense of morality. We never saw eye to eye. He ran a sex trafficking ring, bringing on girls from Albania, Lithuania and other places. He sold them for sex and charged his punters for the pleasure of killing."

"And this man's name?"

"Donny."

"Donny?" said Luan.

"Donny Cartwright."

Luan stepped in front of Harvey with his head cocked in interest and Adeo's eyes bored into Harvey.

"I saved the girls and took Donny to the basement where Sergio had boiled."

"Go on." Luan was getting excited.

"I left him there with the girls he had sold. He was torn to shreds by ten angry women who had narrowly escaped death. They emerged from the dark stairs with his blood on their hands and faces. Donny Cartwright had been mutilated beyond recognition."

"There is honour in your story."

Harvey didn't reply.

"You're a cold man, but you have a warm heart." Luan nodded. "You should hope now that Adeo here is not such a storyteller."

He turned to Adeo who hung his head, then raised it and turned to face Harvey like Luan wasn't there.

"I worked once for a man. It was mostly collecting money and breaking bones. But sometimes my partner and I were asked to take care of people, men who got in the way, or who over-stepped the mark. We would make them disappear, quietly and quickly, with little mess."

Harvey held Adeo's gaze as he told the story. Adeo wasn't struggling to remember the details, they were fresh in his mind like they'd hung there waiting to be told.

"Leo was a strong man, a practised killer. He was feared throughout the East End, but he was also one of those men who carried his presence well. He was respected. He was gentle to those who needed a softer touch, but he could be brutal. Leo had this gift. He could make people talk. He'd barely touch them and they would tell us everything we needed to know. He'd deliver death slowly, drawing out the pain and savouring the screams like a king savouring the finest wines. I liked Leo, everybody did. But one day, our boss, a powerful man, called me into his office alone and told me to finish Leo."

"Finish Leo?" asked Luan.

"Kill him. Leo had failed the boss. He had made his own judgment call and allowed a woman who had wronged the family to live; he'd allowed her to escape. The boss found out. Of course, I followed my instruction and lay in wait inside Leo's house, hidden in the darkness of the shadows. I waited all night for him to return, something I was accustomed to. But Leo was a dangerous man. I had one chance, and if I failed, he would have killed me. When he stepped past me in the darkness, I reached out and cut his throat. One slice. No turning back. His wife, Olivia, had been standing behind him. I hadn't seen her."

"That was a mistake," said Luan.

Adeo stared at the ground and nodded. "She fell to her knees and screamed, louder than I ever heard a scream before, piercing and haunting. She was beautiful, even in her anguish. Leo had been the envy of the firm." Adeo looked up and stared at Luan. "I cut her throat too. I laid her on top of Leo so they may die together with the knife in her hands, and I ran." Adeo let his head fall back. Harvey saw a thin shiny trail of tears stream from his eye. "A small girl sat on a chair by the front door beside a baby in a hamper."

Harvey snatched his head up and lurched at Adeo. His rope snapped tight. "You bastard!" he shouted, and swung his legs to connect with Adeo. But Adeo stepped away to the limit of his rope out of Harvey's reach.

"*Untie me*, Luan," snarled Harvey. "Untie me *now*."

"You're in no position to-"

"*I said untie me.*" Spit flew from Harvey's lip. His wild eyes were wide with anger and hatred.

"I picked up the children, and I ran from the house."

"No!" screamed Harvey. "Stop."

Neighbours had heard her scream. They gathered in the street and saw me run from the house," continued Adeo.

"No more, you bastard," Harvey yelled. He was snatching at the rope, pulling it in all directions, looking for a weakness in the fixing.

"I like this," said Luan. "Carry on, Adeo." He looked enthralled at Harvey's rage.

"I was known to the people that saw me leave the scene. We all were; we ran the place. My brother took the rap for me, and then travelled back to Portugal, while I hid in Britain with some allies far away from this place."

Harvey fell limp and hung from his bindings. His arms stretched awkwardly upwards. His head hung towards the cold, hard ground.

"Is that your story, Adeo?" asked Luan.

Adeo nodded.

"So, you are a coward? You ran and let your brother take the blame. Are you ashamed?"

Adeo nodded once more. "If it is my time to die, then it was time to tell my story." Adeo looked at Harvey then let his eyes fall to the floor.

"I have decided," said Luan, "which one of you shall die slowly and painfully and which one of you shall die fast." Luan ran the blade along Harvey's chest and took a long, deep breath.

"Adeo, you will suffer in the most horrific manner of deaths. You shall be opened up and gutted like a fish while you still breathe the air of this world. I shall feed you your own liver."

Adeo inhaled sharply but held his face taught and let his cold stare land on Luan's smiling, chilling expression.

"It has to be me," said Harvey quietly.

"Excuse me?" said Luan. "Did you speak?"

"Let me do it."

## DECOY

# 15

"Reg, this is Melody. Come back."

"I hear you, Melody. Where the bloody hell are you? It's so noisy."

"Well, surprise, surprise, Reg, Jackson has a chopper license."

"Oh no, not again."

"It's okay, Reg, we haven't stolen this one. We're in the air now. Where are we going?"

"Looks like Harvey is heading out to Southend on the East Coast."

"What the hell is he doing there?"

"Maybe he fancied a go on the arcade machines?"

"No, this is wrong, Reg."

"The trackers don't lie, Melody."

"Southend, Jackson," said Melody.

"Any idea what he's driving, Reg?"

"Well, the satellite imagery shows that the Range Rover is missing from the junkyard. So I checked with the car's GPS and can confirm that it is also heading towards Southend."

"He's got style," said Jackson.

"He's out of his mind," said Melody. "Okay, Reg, we'll touch base when we're closer."

"Okay," said Reg. "I'm setting up a beta version of LUCY's mobile app on your phone. Wait a minute then you'll find the icon on your screen. You should be able to get a real-time visual of Harvey's chips."

"Perfect," said Melody. "I'll wait one minute then get back to you if I have any issues."

The A127 was a dual carriageway that ran from Romford out to the East Coast, snaking its way through the Essex countryside. Melody waited a minute as directed by Reg, then found the new app on her smartphone home screen. Reg had made the icon a simple L-shape with a stereotypical, cartoon burglar wearing a stripy shirt and a mask over his eyes hiding behind the L.

The app opened into a typical map view, but a drop-down on the left showed various names that Melody could select. Her name was there along with Jackson's, Reg's and even Frank's. Of course, Harvey's name was there too, so she hit the little check sign next to the names Harvey and Melody. The map showed a waiting sign, then the letters M and H appeared on the screen. H was travelling along the dual carriageway with M approximately two kilometres behind.

"We're close," said Melody to Jackson. "Another two kilo-metres. Let's take it wide and flank him just in case."

Jackson nodded and turned the chopper south-south-east.

"Reg, come back."

"Go ahead."

"LUCY works fine. We're on him now. We'll let you know when we have him on board."

"Copy that, Melody."

"You do not honestly think that I would cut you down and then arm you?" said Luan.

"You don't need to arm me," said Harvey. He spoke from the very pit of his stomach, staring down at the floor in a mix of disbelief and realisation. He'd accepted long ago that it had been Julios who had killed his parents. He had abandoned any subconscious inclination to hold onto his memory. But Harvey had been wrong, misguided, and now the truth had been laid out in front of him. Adeo was the killer. Adeo was the man he'd been hunting all this time. He had stood side by side with Harvey, protecting him, and now hung from chains in a bunker beside him.

"Let me be the one. I've earned it. I accept death. In fact, it couldn't come sooner, but only once I've finished this."

"No," said Luan coldly. "Why?"

"I was that child, Luan. They were my parents." Harvey fixed Luan in his stare. "I've been chasing this man all my life. So if I'm about to die, at least give me the honour of killing him."

"Interesting," said Luan with consideration. "But I have a better idea." He walked to the bench, rolled up the leather pouch that contained his tools and held them under his arm. Luan opened the door and placed the tools outside then stepped back inside the dark room. He pulled his handgun from inside his coat, and spoke loud and clear.

"You will both fight," said Luan, "to the death."

Harvey looked around and saw only the chair as a potential weapon. "The man who stands at the end will be shot dead. Quite painless."

"Are you going to cut us down?" asked Harvey.

"Oh no, this you must figure out yourselves," said Luan. "Good luck, gentlemen." Luan closed the door.

Before the lock had been turned, Harvey caught sight of Adeo's leg reaching out to kick Harvey. Harvey lifted his legs and hung from the bindings. He had to get free. If Adeo broke free before him, he would be killed.

With all his remaining energy, Harvey hung from the rope and chains and hoisted his legs up, so his feet were above him on the concrete ceiling. With all his might, he pushed his legs against the roof. But it was no use; the eye bolt was screwed into the thick concrete. He saw Adeo beside him using his immense weight and working the rope back and forth to create friction. Harvey began to do the same with his feet against the ceiling. Pushing down, he ran the rope back and forth until a thin blue smoke began to form. His arms and shoulders ached and burned from being held up in the air. His wrists started to bleed as they rubbed against the harsh manila bindings. But slowly, fibres in the rope began to break.

Harvey glanced across at Adeo who had worked up a rhythm and was making progress. He chanced a wild kick and his boot connected with Adeo's nose, but he continued undeterred. Determination was set on his face.

Harvey worked harder than before. He knew that when the rope eventually gave way, he would crash head first to the floor, but that was inevitable. He heard the splitting of fibres, but not his own. It was Adeo's rope, who was now frantic. His massive bulk hung from the chains, and smoke rose steadily from the bindings.

Harvey doubled his efforts. He chose a longer action to get the most friction. The blood had gone to his head, and he dizzied with the effort, but something inside pushed him on. Some carnal survival instinct told him that if Adeo broke free first, Harvey would die.

He began to hear his own rope splitting.

Adeo's chains rattled beside him.

Smoke, thick now, rose like a flame.

Adeo growled with the effort.

Harvey's breathing fell in time with his rhythmic action; short, sharp stabs of concentrated breath.

Metal clattered.

Faster.

Concrete dust reached Harvey's nostrils.

He pushed harder with his legs against the ceiling.

Adeo stood beside him. His weight had finally ripped the eye bolt from the ceiling. He stood beside Harvey with his wrists still bound, and a heavy lump of chain swinging from the rope.

Harder.

Adeo swung the chain.

Faster.

The steel ring on the end of the chain connected with Harvey's back. He lost his momentum, and his breath stung. Harvey's legs screamed to drop down and give up. His shoulders burned.

Slam. Another blow to his back from the chain.

Blood from his wrists ran down his arms, and flaps of skin on either hand were held open by the harsh rope.

Crack. His shoulder blade took the brunt of the next blow. He worked the rope faster despite his body screaming in pain. He saw the chain being swung back for another blow then finally the rope gave. Harvey fell to the floor and smashed his forehead on the hard concrete. Somewhere, in some other part of his vision, he saw Adeo swing widely and miss. Harvey rolled; he needed distance. Adeo's chains crashed into the concrete beside his head, and Harvey scrambled to his feet. The blood ran back into his limbs. His wrists stung like fire, and his right eye began to swell from hitting the floor. He ducked another of Adeo's wild swings and charged at the big man, catching him off balance. They both stumbled to the ground and Harvey landed two good head butts before Adeo threw him off like a doll. Adeo's nose was broken, and blood ran out freely down his face. He smiled a cruel smile and licked the blood from his lips.

Harvey grabbed the wooden chair, and prodded the big man like a lion tamer, using the chair to block his swinging chain until Adeo wrapped the chain around its legs and wrenched it out of Harvey's hands.

Then Harvey stopped. He calmed himself. Maybe it was the memory of Julios and the discovery of his innocence; he hadn't killed Harvey's parents. He *had* been a friend. He remembered Julios' words, the same as he had done a thousand times before. *Patience, planning and execution.*

Harvey waited. He dodged Adeo's wild swings. He planned, analysing Adeo's moves until he spotted a weakness. Most large men like Adeo had protective muscle against their internal organs, which rendered kidney shots or any attempt to wind them useless. The key to fighting larger men was the throat or the groin.

Then it happened. Adeo took a wild downward swing that would have smashed Harvey's skull. But Harvey sidestepped, and with an open hand, he jabbed out at Adeo's throat. One fast jab, in and out. Adeo gasped for breath. The human reaction to loss of airflow is panic. Adeo was no different. He reached up to his throat with his eyes opened wide. Harvey reached out again with both hands and forced his thumbs into Adeo's eye sockets. He pushed hard until both thumbs were up to his knuckles inside Adeo's skull. Then Harvey forced the big man against the concrete wall.

Adeo still fought for breath. He tried to grab Harvey, but he was weak with panic. His attempts were futile. Harvey lifted the big man's head and delivered a headbutt with no effect. He tried again and again until Adeo's nose was a flattened mess on his face. Harvey removed his thumbs. Adeo's eyes searched around uselessly. He was blinded, stumbling and regaining his breath, when Harvey struck once more.

The final blow was a perfect uppercut that dislodged Adeo's jaw. The big man fell against the wall with his arms up in defence.

Harvey smashed the wooden chair against the wall and picked up one of the broken legs, an eighteen-inch length of smooth wood that had been lathed perfectly round. One end was broken, pointed and sharp. Harvey stretched his neck right then left, each time waiting for the satisfying click of the joints. Then he moved closer to Adeo who held onto the wall with panic etched across his blind face.

Harvey stood over Adeo in the dim light. He felt power surging through him as if it was fed from Adeo's diminishing will to live. Adeo dropped to his knees then fell forwards onto all fours. Harvey placed his foot on Adeo's back and forced him to the ground. The big man gave little resistance.

"You should know, Harvey," rasped Adeo. "You should know that your father was a good man."

"I have no doubt, Adeo."

"Do you ever wonder where you get your talent, Harvey?"

"Your brother trained me."

"Yes, he trained you, as he trained me also. But you have something inside you, a fire, Harvey. It's in your blood."

"I was just a kid."

"You were a little monster, Harvey. You were always wild. But you were also fair and warm-hearted. It's from Leo I think."

"It didn't do *him* much good, did it?"

"He died well, Harvey. It is a game we all play, a line we all walk. But we know that one day death will step from the shadows."

"Am *I* standing in the shadows now, Adeo?"

"No, Harvey, you are not. But then, you were never one to follow the rules."

"Are you ready, Adeo?"

"It was John that gave the order, Harvey," said Adeo. "Remember that. John gave the order, but it was me that carried you away." Adeo's eyes searched blindly for Harvey. Then, as if accepting defeat, they cast down to the floor. Adeo lowered himself to his knees and hung his head. "Do as you must."

Harvey pulled Adeo's head back by his hair and placed the chair leg in his mouth. "Bite."

Adeo closed his mouth around the leg. His teeth bit into one end of the chair leg. The other end rested on the floor. Adeo knew what was coming.

"I'll always remember it, Adeo."

Harvey stamped down on the back of Adeo's head and forced the chair leg up into Adeo's brain.

———

"There he is, Jackson, ten o'clock. He's pulling off the main road."

"Where does that take him?"

"Nowhere. Looks to me like a dead end, just an old farm."

"Okay, I'm going to take us down lower."

Jackson eased forward on the collective, which changed the pitch of the blades. The chopper descended slightly, and Jackson maintained an altitude of fifty metres, swinging the bird around to the car's right-hand side.

"I can't see much," said Melody. "Looks like he has a passenger."

"Unless he's tied up in the boot."

"The thought crossed my mind too, Jackson. But I don't believe it. Whatever is happening, Harvey is in control."

The car came to a stop at the edge of a field, and Jackson descended more to bring the chopper down on the grass beside it. The passenger window rolled down, and the muzzle of an AK-74 thrust out and began to let off short bursts at the helicopter.

"Whoa, abort," said Melody. A few of the rounds glanced off the fuselage.

"Holy crap. What did you say about Harvey being in control?"

Two men climbed out the SUV and took aim at the helicopter. Jackson banked right and took the chopper well clear of the gun's effective range.

"Now what?"

"Put me down somewhere. The only way out is back along that lane, so get me in front of them."

"You asked for it."

Jackson took the chopper down in the field a few metres from where the narrow lane met the busy dual carriageway. Melody saw the lights of the car turning in the distance; it was coming back. She took a quick glance at the LUCY app on her phone and saw that Harvey's tracker was stationary where the car had stopped. "Harvey is still up there. Go check he's okay, I'll take care of these guys." Melody cocked the MP5, slammed the door and ran off towards the lane to cut the car off, leaving Jackson to cut through the field to get Harvey.

She stood in the tree line as the headlights grew closer. Then as the car approached, she stepped out and fired off a full magazine in three round bursts. The left-hand tyres blew out, the windscreen shattered; the car veered off the track and slammed into the deep drainage ditch that ran alongside it.

A silence hung in the frigid air.

Melody quickly replaced the magazine and stepped closer, shifting the aim of her weapon between the driver and the passenger.

"Out of the car, now," she yelled.

There was no reply. The driver was slumped over the wheel and angry steam rolled across the front of the car.

Suddenly, the passenger door opened and an automatic weapon emerged.

Melody dropped to the ground, rolled, aimed, and fired three rounds. She rolled once more, keeping her eyes on the car. Wild automatic fire shot high into the sky with bright muzzle flash as Melody's shots pinned the man against the car. Melody pushed the weapon's selector to full automatic, aimed slowly, then emptied the magazine into his body.

The shooting stopped. Melody lay still. Gravity overcame the dead gunman; he buckled and slumped awkwardly to the muddy ground.

Melody slowly rose to a crouch and made her way carefully to the rear of the car. She kicked the man's weapon away and surveyed the damage. The driver had been hit in the neck and the chest; he stared at her with dead eyes. The second man was unrecognizable.

Her phone began to ring, Harvey's number flashed up on the small screen. A wave of relief washed over her as she hit the green *answer* button.

"Harvey, thank god you're okay," said Melody, "we thought-"

"Melody, it's Jackson."

Silence.

"There's nothing here but a pile of Harvey's clothes, and his phone."

"He's not there?" she asked.

"I searched everywhere," replied Jackson, "he's nowhere to be seen."

"Oh no, Jackson," Melody's heart began to pound and her throat clenched at the possibilities that ran through her mind. "We need to go, and we need to go fast."

"Where?" replied Jackson, he began sprinting back to the helicopter holding the phone to his ear.

"It's a decoy," said Melody, as she too began to head back to the chopper, "he's still there at the plant, and if he's lost everything, he's in a lot of trouble."

# THE LION'S DEN

Bobby 'Bones' Carnell stood at the bar of the Pied Piper with Doug and Trev. He drank his scotch and soda down in one hit and put the glass on the bar.

"Yes please, Lee, and a beer for the boys too."

"Cheers, Bobby," said Doug. "So no news then?"

"Yeah, loads of news, Doug," said Bobby. "It's a fast moving world out there. Gerry and the big fella have apparently annihilated the Albanians, and Dom has moved into their pubs. We've regained some lost ground. So the future's looking bright, mate."

"And Gerry?" asked Doug.

"What are you two an item or something, Doug?" replied Bobby. "That's the second time you asked about him."

"I just thought he would be an asset to the firm, Bobby. He's pretty handy."

"He's a fucking liability is what he is, Doug, my old son." Bobby took a large mouthful of his drink and put his glass back down neatly on the coaster. "Doesn't follow orders, he's a wildcard. Sure, he's handy to have in a row, but when the game is strategy, I need men who do then ask, not ask then do their own thing. He's too bloody unpredictable."

"So are we going to just forget about him?"

"Oh no, Dougy. I'm not that callous. He did, after all, get me the Albanian, which in turn gave us the name of the boss and their whereabouts."

"So we're going to take care of him then? I know he's hard up at the minute, that's all."

"I didn't realise you were so soft, Doug."

"I'm not soft, Bobby. It's just that, well, he did us a turn. I thought the least we can do is slip him a few quid."

"Tell me, Doug, how much do you know about this Gerry fellow?"

"Not much. He was pretty quiet."

"And how many times did he come in here?"

"A few."

"And he drank with you every time?"

"Yeah, he was a decent bloke."

"So, right now, some bloke we don't know is out there somewhere, and knows a lot more about us that we do about him?"

"Well," said Doug, "if you put it like that."

"I do put it like that, Doug. If the Albanians haven't chopped him up into little pieces and fed him to the fish, your first job is to find him and take care of it. Is that understood?"

"Ah, that's a bit-"

"Is that understood, Doug?"

Doug paused. "Yeah, Bobby, I get it."

"Good. The firm is expanding, Doug. Now's a good time for you to move up the ranks a bit. Dom has got his own firm in North London now. I need a good right-hand man down here. Stop being a pussy and show me what you're made of."

The door to the pub opened and a familiar but unwelcome face walked in. The ambient noise fell quiet.

"Bobby, you might want to see this," uttered Doug under his breath.

"Carnell," said John Cartwright.

"You're brave coming here alone, John," said Bobby, turning and leaning on the bar.

"I hope that's not a threat, Bobby?" said John. "What're you going to do, slot me in front of all these people?"

"They're all friends, John. They won't see anything if I tell them to look away."

"Besides," said John, ignoring the power play, "while all this is going on, I'd say having an open channel is pretty healthy. Your boy is out there with mine."

"I hear they were welcomed with open arms."

"They were welcomed, Bobby. I don't think open arms is an accurate evaluation."

"As long as they get the job done, John. That's all that counts, isn't it?"

"You heard from your guy? Gerry, wasn't it?"

"Yeah it was Gerry, and no, we haven't heard from him. You heard from him, Doug?"

"No, Bobby," replied Doug. "Not a little-"

"You don't seem too bothered by it, Bobby," said John.

"Well, he'll be well remembered, John. I was just telling Doug here that we should get a plaque engraved and put up behind the bar." He sipped at his scotch. "Drink, John?"

"No, Bobby."

"Lee, brandy, three ice cubes please," said Bobby, ignoring John's answer. "You heard from the big bloke then, John?"

"No, but I will, I'm sure of it."

"Is that right, John? And what if you don't? What if it's all gone a bit Pete Tong and they're both cut up into little pieces?"

"Then, Bobby," spat John, "you and I will need another plan. That would give the Albanians all the confidence they need to start spreading their dirty little feet."

"Oh, I wouldn't worry about that, John."

"And why's that?"

"Well, right now, all the Albanians have is a few old junk-yards and some pubs in North London that nobody else wants. Plus probably some protection and knowing them, they've also got their dirty little mitts in some dirty little brothels as well. But that's not my cup of tea, John."

"You've moved in?"

"Early bird and all that, John," said Bobby with a smug grin.

"You want to make sure someone doesn't knock that grin off your mug, Bobby. It doesn't do to try and get one over on me."

Doug put his beer down. "You need to watch your mouth, John."

"Am I talking to you? No. You'll know when I'm talking to you because I'll look at you. I might even throw you a biscuit and pat you on the head too, so shut up and sit back down."

Doug looked at Bobby, who shook his head. "Sit down, Doug. Listen, John. There's no need for all this. I was faster off the mark than you. Maybe it's time you got out of all this. You've done well, you're well known, respected even. Maybe you're a bit long in the tooth for it, mate. It's a young man's game."

John downed his drink and put the glass back down on the polished wood. He moved closer to Bobby and spoke quietly.

"We either do this together, Bobby, or not at all. I'm in your manor, I respect that. But do not overstep your mark."

"Goodbye, John," said Bobby. "Shut the door on the way out, will you?"

"Is that the way you want things to be?"

Bobby didn't reply.

John turned and walked out the pub. He left the doors open.

"He's got to go, Doug," said Bobby.

"You're going to off John Cartwright?"

"No, Doug, my old son," replied Bobby, "*you* are going to off John Cartwright. Now close the door, will you? It's bloody freezing."

Doug took in the statement and walked to the doors. Killing John Cartwright would go down in history within the confines of the criminal world in which they operated. The man had survived countless attacks and had run most of the East End for longer than many of Bobby's men had been alive.

Doug pushed the door closed, but as he turned, the doors were kicked open again behind him. Two men stepped inside. The first shot Doug in the face; the second emptied his handgun into Bobby 'Bones' Carnell. They looked around the pub. The few drinkers sat in booths with their mouths hanging open. There was no other reaction. No more of Bobby's men.

The two men stepped back outside and climbed into the waiting van. The first man dialled a number on his phone.

"Jasper?"

"Boss, it's done. He's down."

"Good work. Get the boys and go seize his assets. It's time people started knowing that John Cartwright is still around. I've been laying low too long."

"Nicely done," said Luan. "I didn't think it would be you still standing."

Harvey didn't reply. Luan was talking through a little slot in the heavy steel door.

"It's almost a shame to kill you. You fight well."

Harvey leaned against the wall. He was ready. It had taken him more than twenty years to find every man on his list. But he'd done it, and now found himself with two more names to add.

Someone had shot Julios two years ago during a gun deal with the Thomsons. Harvey had chased them, but they got away. The man may take some finding. John Cartwright had also been placed on his list, a name Harvey never thought would be there. But he'd given the order; John was responsible for the death of Harvey's parents and knew he must pay the price.

Harvey thought about the story John used to tell him about his parents, how he'd found Hannah and Harvey on a bench seat in his pub. Harvey had been in a hamper with a note. His sister had sat next to him. The note had said that his parents had killed themselves. John had told the story verbatim for years. But now Harvey had discovered the truth and he could see why John had lied. His father had been a dangerous man, and Harvey had inherited his keen sense of survival, his raw power and ferocity. John had known all along that he had been breeding a killer.

And now that killer was about to turn on him.

The unmistakable thumping of a helicopter beat the air above the bunker and Harvey tore himself away from his thoughts of how to kill John.

"Who is this?" asked Luan.

"Are you expecting company?" asked Harvey.

The door opened, and Luan stood with his handgun pointing at Harvey.

"Do not try to make any moves. I will cut you down. I see I have toyed for too long with you."

"If you're going to point that at me, you better know how to use it, Luan."

"I was firing guns before your daddy's vermin seed found its spawn," spat Luan. "Out, and keep your hands where I can see them."

Harvey stepped out of the dark room and into the night. The cold bit into his skin and his bare feet sank in the thick brown mud.

Harvey felt Luan's fillet knife against his throat and the gun in the small of his back. He was pro; nobody could fend off both attacks. If Harvey reached for the knife, Luan would fire the gun. If he reached for the gun, Luan would slash his throat.

The chopper hung in the air fifty metres away. Harvey heard Jackson's voice loud and tinny over the tannoy fixed to the underside of the helicopter's fuselage.

"Let him go, Duri. We'll take it easy on you."

The bright spotlights fixed on either side of the chopper's windshield shone directly on Harvey and Luan, blinding them both. Only the faint outline of the rear rotor could be seen on the edge of the silhouette. Jackson fought the controls against the strong wind and descended some more. The slight variation in the helicopter's stability gave Harvey a brief glimpse of Melody. She was in the back with the door open and one foot on the skid. Presumably, her Diemaco was aimed at Luan.

Harvey battled in his head. Knife or gun?

The knife would surely kill him; the gun needed reaction time.

"It's not so easy, I'm afraid," shouted Luan.

"Don't make me do this," Melody shouted back.

"I won't make you do anything."

Harvey felt the blade cut skin.

"Make your move," Luan cried at the chopper.

Harvey reached up and wrenched Luan's hand from his throat, twisting it away then bending over in one smooth motion, pulling Luan over his back. The handgun flailed in the air as Luan fought to stay upright and tumbled over Harvey's shoulder in a slick judo throw.

Luan landed, rolled and stood in one smooth motion. He lifted the gun to point it at Harvey. He opened his mouth to say something, and the front of his head exploded.

---

Melody stepped down to the ground. She aimed her weapon around and cleared the area before stepping up to Harvey.

"Cold?" she asked.

Harvey didn't reply.

"Who's this?" asked Melody.

"Luan Duri," said Harvey. "The main man."

"And Adeo?"

"Inside."

"Alive?"

Harvey didn't reply.

"So no survivors?"

"None worth mentioning," replied Harvey. "Mind if I get some clothes before we carry on this chat, Melody?"

"I didn't think of you as the shy type, Harvey."

"Let's go. Whose chopper?"

"Jackson called in a favour."

"Don't suppose it has a spare change of clothes inside?"

"Want my jacket?" Melody said with a smirk.

"No. Luan won't be needing this anymore." Harvey began to remove the long coat from Luan Duri's dead body.

"You're going to take a dead man's coat?"

"Melody, I'm naked and it's November."

A few minutes later, Harvey joined Melody and Jackson in the chopper.

"Right, let's get this bird back to Hackney," said Jackson. "I think we just about pushed our luck here."

"Headquarters, Jackson."

"No time, Harvey," said Melody.

"Headquarters, Jackson," said Harvey. "You can land on the roof."

"Harvey, Frank wants to talk to us before we do anything else," said Melody. "Let's get this back to Hackney first, eh?"

"Do I have to flag a cab?"

"What's the rush?" asked Melody. "We got Duri."

"We got Duri, but..." Harvey couldn't talk. If he mentioned John Cartwright, Melody would know instantly that he'd go on a rampage. "They're still out there. The firm will wonder where I am."

"Bobby Bones?"

"Yeah, he's a bit of loose cannon that one."

"So not John Cartwright then."

Harvey didn't reply.

"Harvey, something has happened. What is it?"

"Jackson, can you get me back to base, mate?" said Harvey, ignoring Melody's question.

"Not leaving me much choice in the matter, are you?"

Harvey stared out the window.

"What happened in there, Harvey?" asked Melody.

Harvey didn't reply.

"Okay, save it. But we'll talk back at HQ." Melody was turned in her seat. She put her hand on his leg. "I'm your friend, remember?" She remembered that he was naked under the long coat and took her hand away. "Just don't bottle it up. Let me help you, Harvey."

"You wouldn't get it, Melody."

"Maybe, but try me. See if I do get it, and I if I do, I'll help you, whatever it is. Alright?"

Harvey turned and stared at her. "Do we still have those two muppets at HQ?"

"Ginger?"

"Yeah."

"Yeah, they're still there," said Melody. "Frank has been on at them. They won't talk."

"Yes they will," said Harvey. "We just need to ask the right questions."

# 17

# THE BEAST AWAKENS

HARVEY AND MELODY STEPPED OUT OF THE HELICOPTER onto the roof of the team headquarters. The wind tore off the river, whipping at Harvey's coat and biting into his skin. A small door led them to the washrooms, and another took them to the main area beside Reg's workstation.

Harvey walked straight to his desk where he kept a sports holdall with a change of clothes.

"Good evening," said Reg. "You're home early."

"Hey, Reg," said Melody, eying Harvey. "What's the news?"

"Oh you know, this and that. Nothing as exciting as what your news will be. Do tell." Reg sat back in his reclining leather office chair waiting for Melody to fill him in on all the details.

Melody took a glance across at the two men handcuffed to the pillar. "Let's talk in a bit, Reg. Where's Frank?"

"I'm here," said Frank. He was stood on the mezzanine floor looking down at Melody. He had a serious look on his face and spoke quietly. "Debrief in ten minutes. Get a coffee, do what you need to do, and get yourself into the mess." He disappeared into his office.

Harvey finished dressing. He tossed the long coat onto the back of his desk chair, walked over to Melody's desk and pulled a thirty-metre length of climbing rope from where it hung on the wall then stopped at Reg's desk.

"Keys."

"What keys?"

Harvey didn't reply.

"Oh, you mean the keys to the handcuffs? Sure here they are." Reg pulled open his desk drawer, but before he could lift the keys out, Harvey's hand was inside the drawer. Harvey strode over to the two men. He formed a loop in the end of the rope and put it around Ginger's neck before unlocking the handcuffs. The driver sat looking up at Harvey looming over them with a scared look on his face. Then he watched as Harvey dragged Ginger away.

"Reg, doors please."

Reg looked at Melody, silently asking if he should open them. Melody nodded reluctantly and watched the top floor to make sure Frank wasn't watching.

Harvey continued to drag Ginger across the smooth screed floor and out into the night. The man struggled to his feet and was led along the walkway to the riverside. His damaged foot from where Harvey had shot him earlier had been cleaned and dressed in a bandage. Without stopping, Harvey hoisted Ginger over the railings and held him above the raging river below. Iron rungs were fixed into the side of the river wall for the men who serviced the Thames Barrier so they could get in and out of boats. Ginger's undamaged foot stood precariously on the edge of one of the slippery rungs.

"Where's John?"

"John?"

"John Cartwright."

"I don't know. Don't let me fall, please. It's just a job. I didn't-"

"I need an address."

"I don't have an-"

Harvey let go but allowed the rope to play through his hands. Ginger splashed down into the river, and the immense current immediately dragged him downstream. The rope pulled taught, and Ginger fought hard to keep from going under. Harvey dragged him back to the side, where Ginger's frozen hands clung to the rungs.

Harvey pulled up on the rope, forcing Ginger to climb unsteadily up the slippery, iron ladder.

"Where?" said Harvey when Ginger had reached the top. Harvey held the rope tight with one hand and held Ginger by the scruff of his neck with the other. Ginger coughed up some river water, and let it run down his face.

"He'll kill me. You don't know him like I do."

Without warning, Harvey landed his forehead on Ginger's nose.

"I know him better than anyone. You've got three seconds. Three."

"No, please."

"Two."

"I can't."

"One."

"Okay, stop."

---

Harvey finished fixing Ginger back to the pillar alongside the driver and took the stairs up to the mess where the team held their meetings. Frank was already stood at the head of the room and Melody had taken her place by the coffee machine.

She held a coffee between both hands, savouring the warmth of the cup. Reg sat on one of the two couches playing on his phone.

"How long until Jackson is back?" asked Frank, ignoring Harvey's entry.

"He'll be another thirty minutes. He'll be coming from Hackney," said Melody.

"Okay, well let's start without him. I'll fill him in later."

Frank sat on the edge of the large dining table that served as the meeting table. In all Harvey's time there, he hadn't seen anybody actually sit and eat there.

"I'll keep it as brief as I can," began Frank. "The chief has been on to me. Stone, can you tell me who you've been talking to? What firm is it? Just to clarify."

"Carnell."

"Bobby Carnell?"

"Yeah, you knew that."

"Just for the record, that's all," said Frank. "In the Pied Piper pub? Am I correct?"

Harvey didn't reply.

"Am I correct, Stone?"

Harvey nodded.

"Bobby 'Bones' Carnell was shot dead in the Pied Piper this evening. Anything you want to tell me?"

"Not really."

"So it wasn't you?"

"No, Frank, I was busy having the life kicked out of me in a concrete bunker buried in some junkyard." Harvey pointed at his swollen eye.

"The chief told me, and I'll paraphrase, the team is creating too many toe tags and not enough arrests."

The room was silent. The chief had the power to shut the unit down. The team had already had several warnings following previous cases and were told to bring more suspects in. The chief had said they were abusing their powers.

"Fourteen men have been found dead in the Ilford scrap yard, Stone," said Frank. "Fourteen?"

Harvey didn't reply.

"Are you not capable of *arresting* anybody?"

"You brought me in to do what you can't do, and I'm doing it. If there's a problem just say the word."

Frank looked disapprovingly at Harvey. "Where's Luan Duri?"

"Lying face down in the mud in Bow."

"Dead?"

"That was me, sir," said Melody. "He was about to execute Harvey."

"Well you should have bloody let him," barked Frank. "We haven't had *one* arrest worth anything in this investigation. Those two downstairs are nobodies. Crime isn't going to come grinding to a halt by taking *them* off the street, is it? We probably can't pin anything on them anyway. Do you see what I'm saying here? We need to do more police work. Leave the SAS crap to the bloody SAS."

The room was silent once more.

"So where does that leave us?"

"Just one more firm left. Seems like somebody did all the hard work for us, sir," said Melody.

"I want John Cartwright in handcuffs and with a pulse. I don't care how you do it, but I want him." Frank glared at Harvey with a look that told Harvey that he didn't care about the relationship between him and Cartwright. "Are you up for this, Stone?"

Harvey stared at Frank. He pushed off the wall where he'd been leaning and stepped over to him.

"Have you any idea what I've been through tonight, Frank?"

"Yes, I can see by the body bags."

"You need knocking down a few pegs, standing there in your nice suit with your hot coffee dishing out *I wants*. I've had enough of it, Frank. I've been shot at, hunted down, had guard dogs set on me, stripped naked, tortured and beaten. Then the final straw was that I was this close, Frank." Harvey held up his finger and thumb an inch apart. "I was this close to being executed, and you expect me to stand here and listen to you dribble on about how there's too many toe tags and not enough arrests? Why don't *you* get out there and see how you get on? These men are dangerous. They don't just put their hands up and let you put the cuffs on, Frank. They fight back. They shoot. They do anything they can to survive another day." Harvey spoke softly. "So finish your nice hot coffee. Go back to your nice, warm office, and stick that in your crappy little report."

Harvey stepped away and opened the door to head out.

"Where are you going, Stone?" asked Frank.

Harvey stopped, turned and glared at Frank. "I'm going to get John Cartwright, and if you want him alive, you'd better go out and get your hands dirty."

"Stone, if you do this, it's over. I can't protect you."

"You're right, Frank," said Harvey. "If I do it, it's over."

"How do you plan on finding him?"

"Easy," said Harvey. "*I* know where he is."

# 18

# HEAD HONCHO

"Tenant, I want Stone on that screen, and as soon as he steps out of line, we call it in. No more games. This isn't a bloodbath. We're supposed to be police."

"He's only got one tracker left, sir, his bike," replied Reg.

"And where's his bike?"

"Currently doing one hundred and ten miles an hour down the A13."

"Well, where's all his other chips? We put one in his neck, didn't we? What the bloody hell happened to that?"

"Duri cut it out, sir. Took his phone off him too."

"And his jacket? Tell me we have one in his jacket."

"Nope," said Reg. "Looks like he pulled that out when he came back."

Frank turned to Ginger who was sat shivering on the floor cuffed to one of the upright pillars that supported the mezzanine. "You. What did you tell him?"

Ginger looked away, then turned back to Frank. "I d-didn't tell him anything."

Frank stared hard at the man who was visibly freezing. "Full immunity."

Ginger cocked his head.

"You haven't got anything on me anyway so immunity from what exactly?"

"You work for John Cartwright."

"Never heard of him."

"That's strange because we have a gun that matches a double homicide in the Pied Piper that took place earlier today, only moments after John Cartwright left the pub."

Ginger closed his eyes in disbelief. "Is that right?"

"The prints on the weapon match yours exactly, Ginger," lied Frank. "And an eyewitness put your silent mate here on the scene too. He held the door. I could probably get his prints off that too if I needed to." Frank paused. "Do you understand the severity of the situation, Ginger?"

"Yeah, you want me to grass."

"You tell me what you told our friend, and maybe John Cartwright survives," said Frank. "You fail to tell me, and I'll see to it that you spend the next ten years sharing a cell with the biggest, friendliest, and loneliest category A prisoner I can find. He'll warm you up, Ginger."

Ginger hung his head. He cast his eyes up to the man opposite him, Clive, who shook his head and mouthed, "It's not worth it."

"No deal," said Ginger.

Frank stood over him then squatted down beside the pair.

"You both just made the biggest mistakes of your lives."

"It doesn't matter. If we grass on John, our lives won't be worth living anyway."

"If you grass on John, Ginger," spat Frank, "you'll be saving his life. Did you see my friend who just left here? Of course you did, look at you. Have you any idea what he's capable of?"

Ginger sat and looked at the floor. "He won't get away alive." He mumbled.

"You what?" said Frank. "What did you say?"

"You didn't honestly think I'd give him John Cartwright's home address, did you?"

Frank stared in disbelief. Melody strode over to Ginger and kicked him hard in the kidneys. "Where have you sent him?"

Ginger just smiled. Then his shoulders began to bounce as he chuckled to himself.

"Tell me where he's going, Ginger," said Frank gravely.

"Why don't you ask your mate? He'll be strolling through the door right about now. I do hope they don't recognise him." Ginger grinned up at Frank.

Melody leaned down and landed a clean right hook into Ginger's jaw.

---

"Boss, it's Jasper."

"What's the news?"

"We're hitting them hard. I've got three crews out there right now cleaning up. By this time tomorrow, nobody will even remember Bobby Carnell."

"Good work," said John. "Carnell said he'd taken over the Albanian's turf too. What's the name of the guy that wiped his arse, Jasper?"

"Dom, boss."

"Dom, that's it. Okay, it'll be him taking care of North London, and you know what? He can keep it. We've got no interest there. Our roots are here. But we need Dom to know that we're doing him a favour. He might be useful later on."

"Send him a message, Jasper. Find out where Bobby Carnell's body is being stored and get yourself up there."

"Boss?"

John spoke quietly, with a cruel intonation. "Cut his right

hand off and send that to Dom. Tell him to stay up there, and we'll all live happily ever after. But if he tries to stretch his legs in East London again, it'll be the end for him *and* his family."

"There's something poetic about that, boss, considering Carnell's fetish for fingers."

"Yeah, if he's got brains he'll pay attention. He might even become an ally one day. But if he hasn't got brains, and doesn't do what he's told, then that's the gene pool at work."

"The gene pool, *right*."

"Any news on Adeo?"

"Nothing, boss. The Albanians are quiet."

"Ginger said Adeo and that Gerry bloke went to some junkyard the Albanians ran. Said it was a bloodbath."

"You think he's alive?"

"Something tells me he's not, Jasper. Shame, I've known him thirty-something years. But it wouldn't be the first mistake he made."

"I don't believe it," said Jasper.

"What?" asked John.

"What if I told you that Bobby's guy just rocked up here?" said Jasper, pleased with his discovery. "He just parked opposite me in the car park."

"Gerry?"

"Yeah, looks like him. Face like a slapped arse. He's on a motorbike just sitting in the dark outside the Basement Club in Barking. Looks like he's waiting for someone or something. I'll call the boys, and in about ten minutes time he'll be dragged into the back of the van and dumped in the river, boss. Leave it with me. I'll take care of-"

"No," said John, a little too abruptly. "Don't touch him."

"Boss? He might know about Adeo."

"I guarantee he knows about Adeo, Jasper, but do not let the boys anywhere near him. I also guarantee that even if they do succeed in getting him into the van, it'll be him who's dumping them the river. I'll be there in thirty minutes. I do not want him touched."

---

"Let's go, Jackson. We'll take the Audi, it'll be quicker," said Melody.

"Mills," said Frank.

"Sir?"

"A quiet word," said Frank, opening the shutter doors and stepping outside into the frigid air.

"We're already behind him, sir."

Frank gave her a look that told her that the talk was non-negotiable.

They walked slowly towards the river then stopped once they were out of earshot of Jackson and Reg.

"It's a delicate situation, Mills."

"Yeah, but I'm keen to look after Harvey. He's mad right now, but he's an asset, sir."

"He is, Mills. He's good at what he does, but he's a liability."

"Can I speak freely?"

"Always."

"With all due respect, sir, you could have gone easier on him. The night he's had would have probably have killed the pair of us. Your words and tone was the last thing he needed. Harvey is in a position where the most powerful villain out there knows he's up to something. If John finds out that Harvey is working with us, he'll never be able to step foot in East London again."

"Yeah, that's a predicament, alright. You think that's the only reason he's going after Cartwright?"

"What other reason is there? I spoke to him about it, and

there doesn't seem to be a relationship between them."

"I got that impression, but I also got the impression Stone respects him. There's not too many people out there Harvey respects, you know that?"

"Yeah, I do."

"He respects you, Mills. You make a good team."

"I admire his strength and control."

"Control? Did you see him leave here?"

"That wasn't him out of control, that was Harvey taking himself out of a situation. I'd bet money he's found somewhere to sit and think before he acts."

"Patience, planning and execution?"

"Exactly, sir."

"If he kills Cartwright, that's it, you know that?"

"Yeah, you said."

"You don't understand, Mills. If he kills Cartwright, the balance will shift. Cartwright is the glue that holds the world out there together. Ever wonder why nobody holds up the off-licenses or local businesses? Did you ever wonder how, in a place where terrible violence happens nearly every day, old ladies can still leave their homes and go play bingo or collect their pensions? The firms might be a royal pain in the arse for us, but trust me, they keep a lot of the crime down. Now tell me, out of the three firms involved in this investigation, which one is still going strong?"

"Cartwright."

"And of those same three, which one didn't we know of until today?"

"Cartwright."

"Exactly. He's a villain, Mills. But if Harvey takes him away, there'll be chaos as smaller, younger and bloodthirsty firms strive to take control and petty criminals begin to take the piss. We'll have more deaths on our hands than we can deal with. If the chief doesn't shut us down anyway for this fiasco, then he'll shut us down for sure when there's a dead body or two showing up every day."

"I understand, sir."

"If Cartwright dies, I can't go on. I'm on the home run towards retirement. I haven't got it in me to learn a new way of doing things. John Cartwright is the last of the old school villains, Mills."

"And you're the last of the old school cops."

"Exactly. I'm tired, Mills. I want to hand over the reins on a high note. Retire in peace, as it were."

"I get that, sir. However, I also think that maybe the time for people like John Cartwright is over. We don't need the carnage, but maybe some fresh blood might do some good."

Frank raised an eyebrow at Melody's comment. "You should see if my chair is comfortable, Mills."

"Sir?"

"My desk chair, see if it's comfortable. I have a feeling you'll be sitting there sooner than you think."

# THE BEAST LURKS

"WHERE DID IT COME FROM?" ASKED DOM.

"We don't know. Nobody saw anything."

"Cartwright."

"Cartwright is down, Dom. He's barely got enough men to make him a cup of tea."

"No, don't you believe it, mate. Cartwright is playing the game. He's on a rampage. He's got men in every one of our pubs from East Ham to Bow."

"So why send us this?"

"It's a message."

"A message? They could have just called instead of sending Bobby's hand."

"Cartwright is drawing a line in the sand."

"What do you mean?"

"If he wanted us, we'd be laying in some dark street right now or buried in Epping Forest. It's not us he wants. He just wants his manor back."

"So we're stuck up here now? I can't stand this place."

"For the time being, mate," said Dom. "We need to leave

Cartwright alone. Let things settle. We're building up numbers. When the time is right, we'll make our move."

"What about the lunatic? Gerry?"

"Gerry?" asked Dom. His mind had trailed off miles from where he stood. Dom was a strategist. He was thinking about John Cartwright and something his dad had taught him when he'd been a boy. Bullies had ripped his shirt and stolen his lunch money, and he'd wanted to get revenge. His dad had told him to make friends with them; retaliating would be futile. For a young teenage boy full of pubescent emotions, the advice had seemed absurd. But as he thought about Cartwright and the position he now found himself in, the strategy made perfect sense.

John would be an ally, a good ally to have. But the things Bobby had taught Dom countered his father's words. Bobby had groomed Dom for the job he did. When Dom had been much younger, Bobby had shown him first-hand how to deal with someone who stepped on his toes or pushed him too far. Bobby was respected for it.

Dom had two choices, and both had severe consequences. Stay out of the East End, let John Cartwright have his manor back and risk losing all respect from Bobby's men, who were his own men now. Or he could strike while Cartwright's numbers were down and his men spread out. Dom knew that they were taking over Bobby's turf. Now might be the only time he could get in an attack. The choices weighed heavily on his mind.

"The hard nut, Dom."

"Yeah." Dom snapped back to the chat with his friend Cole. "He managed to make a name for himself pretty quick, didn't he?"

"Apparently Bobby liked him. He said he had a certain cold style. Even made the Albanian bloke cry and didn't lay a finger on him."

"Do we know anything else about him?"

"No, Dom. It was Doug that found him and made the introduction. He met him in the Piper apparently."

"When exactly was that?"

"A few days ago. The day after the Dockside Arms was burned down."

"Convenient, don't you think?"

"What're you saying, Dom?"

"I'm saying that I wonder if this Gerry is really who he says he is. Did you see how he spoke to Cartwright? And how he ignored Bobby?"

"He's a hard nut, Dom."

"No, there's more to it than just hard. It's like he was somehow above it all. Like none of it really mattered."

"You reckon it was him that killed Bobby?"

"No, it was two men according to Lee the barman. He didn't say it was Gerry and I'm pretty sure he would have if it was."

"So what are you thinking?"

"I'm thinking a lot, Cole. I'm thinking that this bloke shows up out of the blue. Three or four pubs are burned down, all of which belong to one firm or another. There's blokes being killed left, right and centre and another one had his ears cut off, and I haven't seen one flashing blue light."

Cole jerked his head at Dom in surprise. "You don't think-"

"I don't know for sure. It's just a theory. But it's just a bit odd, that's all. Don't you think?"

"I think you're paranoid, Dom."

"Maybe, Cole. Get word out to the boys, will you? Bobby is dead. I'm taking over."

Cole smiled. "You've got some balls, Dom, I'll give you that."

"Tell them we're meeting in the Rose and Crown tonight."

"You going to give a speech, Dom?"

"No speeches, Cole. Tell them to come tooled up. We're going to pay John Cartwright and his boys a little visit. We'll start with that crappy little club of his, what's it called?"

"The Basement Club."

"Yeah, that's it," said Dom. "I want every bit of firepower we've got."

"I'm going to wipe John Cartwright off the face off the earth."

---

"Call your pet dog off," said the voice on the other end of the phone. Frank was silent. "Did you hear me?"

"I heard you, but the play is rolling. If I call him off, there'll be questions."

"So use your imagination."

"It's too far gone."

"You stand to lose a lot more than I do, Carver. You know that?"

"And if I don't?" said Frank.

"An anonymous phone call to your superiors maybe?"

"You don't have anything on me."

"Phone calls, Frank. Records of our conversations," said the voice. "Plus a certain murder of my friend Mr Parrish."

"He was a wanted murderer. That little incident got me a reward."

"I'm not talking about legal action, Carver."

"Stone?"

"What do you think he'll do if he finds out it was you that killed Julios all along."

Frank gave the question time to settle.

"What makes you so sure he works for me? What makes you think I have any control over him?"

"Oh, Frank, you don't control Harvey Stone. Nobody does. But if you're any good, you can steer him."

"How do you know he works for me?"

John laughed. "Frank, I don't like to blow my own trumpet, but I didn't get where I am without being a *bit* smart. He's a cop. Harvey very likely didn't go to police training after being almost invisible for most of his life. If he turned, then he was coerced. And if he was coerced then, my friend, there's only one dirty cop I can think of who would try a stunt like that. As soon as I found out it was you who shot Edgar and Harvey had gone to the dark side, so to speak, well, two and two, Frank. Keep your friends close and your enemies closer. That's what you've been doing all this time, isn't it?"

"What do you think he'll do if gets his hands on you? You did, after all, have his parents killed. I doubt he'll even give you time to talk."

"What makes you think I killed his parents?"

"You're not the only one who can count two and two. Harvey told me how you used to tell him the same old story. How you found him and Hannah-"

"In my bar, on a seat." John finished. "I'm his father, Frank. I'm sure I can appeal to his good nature. That puts me in a pretty strong position. With one phone call, I can have you arrested. You'll lose your pension and probably go away for a spell at Her Majesty's pleasure. I'm sure you'll be welcomed inside, Frank. Lots of old friends who'll want to say hi. Or I can set Harvey on the right path. You know, tell him a few truths about his dirty cop boss. I'm sure he'll go easy on you. Maybe he'll even make it quick. But I doubt it."

There was a silence as both men played the possibilities out in their heads.

"So this is goodbye, Frank. May the best man win."

John Cartwright disconnected the call.

Frank walked slowly towards the doors to headquarters.

"Mills, keep me informed," said Frank.

Melody was loading the Audi with her peli-cases. One contained her MP5, another had her Diemaco sniper rifle, and the last had a mixture of surveillance equipment. Boon was following her around the workspace and sniffing at the boxes.

"Will do, sir. You heading home?"

"It's been a long day, Mills. This old dog needs some rest. And that old dog needs a walk." Frank gestured at Boon.

"He'll get one soon enough."

Frank hesitated, looked her in the eye, and smiled weakly. He glanced around the headquarters then turned and walked to his car.

Melody watched him leave then called Jackson again. "We're moving."

"Harvey is outside The Basement club in Barking. At least his bike is. Obviously, I can't tell if he's actually gone in for a dance or not."

"We'll know soon enough, Reg," said Melody. "Listen, did Frank seem off to you?"

"You mean did he seem grumpy and miserable? Isn't that normal?"

"No, I mean..." Melody stumbled for words. "I don't know. He said some weird things."

"Like what?"

"I can't say. But can you keep an eye on him?"

"Yeah, sure. Want me to listen to his calls?"

"No, Reg, just, I don't know what I'm saying, sorry. I'm tired, and nothing seems normal anymore."

"Normal?" Reg laughed. "This *is* normal, Melody."

"Let's go," called Jackson.

Melody climbed into the passenger seat of the saloon and leaned out to pull the door closed. "Reg?"

Reg spun in his seat to face Melody. He smiled as if reading her thoughts.

"Thanks, Reg," she said.

---

Harvey hated the loud, obnoxious beat of dance music. It dulled his senses. Mixed with the dark shadows of the basement club, his ability to control risk, make a plan and execute it was narrowed. But Harvey had no plan other than to find John Cartwright and take him down.

One of John's men had seen Harvey in the car park. He'd sat watching Harvey. Harvey had seen the faint glow of a mobile phone against the man's face and was sure he was sending an update on Harvey, maybe to John himself. It didn't matter. In fact, it helped Harvey. John now knew where to find him. Two things could happen. John would somehow know that Harvey had turned, and was undercover; he'd be torn to pieces. Or John would find him and they'd talk, then Harvey would kill John. He couldn't see any other option. Nobody in John's world could know about Harvey's involvement with what was essentially the police. Official or unofficial, it would make no difference to hardened criminals.

Harvey found a small booth in the corner of the club. It was on the ground floor with the main entrance in full view and a staff door to Harvey's left. He felt the stares from the men that prowled the room. He'd definitely been recognised.

Opposite and to the side of Harvey were three larger booths. It was the type of seating shown in the gangster movies that Harvey's foster brother, Donny, had been thrilled by as a child. Glamorous looking women would be sat either side a coke-sniffing, over-confident hoodlum who would be drinking champagne and slipping folded wads of cash to staff, valets and girls every five minutes. The scene in front of

Harvey was very different. Each booth sat five or six men, all holding bottles of beer, smoking cigarettes and trying to look as tough as possible. They were joined by the guy Harvey had seen sitting in his car on the phone. In a series of silent gestures, nods and headshakes, the men in the room decided not to make a move on Harvey.

It amused Harvey to watch the scene play out. He could see what they were doing, he understood what they said, and he realised the reasons why. They might as well have just spoken out loud. John Cartwright was clearly on his way.

Harvey played out the plan in his head. He would take John away from the club somewhere quiet, somewhere they could talk. Harvey had questions; John would give the answers. Then Harvey would let him die. It would be quick. John deserved that for the way he'd raised Harvey and Hannah. He'd provided as well as he could for them. But for the lies, the deceit and for killing his parents, John must die.

John Cartwright strode through the main doors at the front of the club and grinned at the girls who flashed their smiles and flicked their over-sized eyelashes his way. He was in his element, thought Harvey. He'd always been one for the women. When Harvey's foster mother had left John, a series of blonde bombshells enjoyed his company. They typically spent more time in the washroom racking up lines than they did with the old man. But the next day, he always had a spring in his step.

There was no eye contact between John and Harvey as John made his way through the room, stopping at any table he passed to introduce himself or greet acquaintances. That's all they were, acquaintances. Men like John Cartwright didn't have friends. They just knew people, the right people.

"Mind if I sit?" asked John, finally reaching Harvey's booth.

"It's *your* seat."

John slipped into the small booth and nodded at the group of men sat opposite. Harvey remained silent. He followed John's eyes to the men, and then back to John. A few seconds later, a brandy with three ice cubes arrived at the table. It was served on a new cardboard coaster with a serviette folded in a neat triangle next to it. A small dish containing three olives finished the demonstration of power and control.

"So," began John, "Gerry, is it?"

"What's a name?"

"Where for art thou, Gerry?"

"Seemed like a safer name to use than Harvey Stone."

"What happened to France? You were always dead keen on France. Thought you'd stay out there."

"Something called me back."

"I'm guessing it wasn't Bobby Carnell that called you back, Harvey."

"It's complex."

"Try me."

"You wouldn't understand."

John Cartwright sat for a moment in silence. He studied Harvey as only a father can. "I'm proud of you, Harvey."

"What is it you're proud of?"

"Just you, mate," replied John. "Your strength, your will. It's infectious."

Harvey didn't reply.

"So, to business then, shall we?"

"Business?"

"I presume that *is* why you've come to see me? To have a go at me on behalf of Bobby Carnell?"

"Bobby can go to hell, John."

"Thought you two were pals?"

"Not really. He's a means to an end."

"That's lucky, Harvey."

"Lucky for who?"

"You, Harvey."

"Why's it lucky for me?"

"Because I shot him earlier."

Harvey didn't reply.

John sipped at his drink like he'd just told Harvey that school was cancelled the next day.

"So it's just you then? You won."

"Did I? Win, that is?"

"Carnell is dead and the Albanians won't be giving anyone more trouble for the foreseeable. You cleaned up, John. Congratulations."

"Yeah well, I'm not exactly singing and dancing about it just yet."

"What's the problem?"

An explosion rocked the room. The sharp crack of the detonator was followed by a deafening boom that rocked Harvey's eardrums. The two swinging front doors were torn off their hinges, and the tables surrounding the grand entrance to the club were blown across the room. Lights blew out and, just for a moment, the scene played out in slow motion for Harvey.

Bright headlights focused on the entrance, blinding anyone who tried to run out of the club, which had begun to smoke and smoulder. Flames were building in several small fires, and smoke was already beginning to fill the room.

Silhouetted against the bright entrance were the legs and torsos of men who stormed the club. John's men in the booths opposite Harvey sprung from their seats and reached for weapons, bottles, knives, chairs, anything they could find. But the attackers were prepared. Shots rang out in a riot of recoil and frantic untrained firing. Many of the men had apparently seen too many films and emptied a full clip into the smoke and confusion. Girls fell to the floor, cut down in the crossfire. Wrong place, wrong time.

Within moments, the attackers were moving towards the rear of the club. Harvey instinctively ducked John's head down. When the gunfire had passed, he wrenched him from the booth to his feet.

Covering John, Harvey turned and kicked in the staff door. There was a cloakroom on Harvey's left and kitchens to his right. He knew that every kitchen had to have a fire exit, so barged inside to the shock of two staff. He held John's head low, and kicked his way through the fire doors. Immediately, the flash of a muzzle and the sound of automatic gunfire traced a line of bullets towards Harvey. They'd been waiting for people to burst through the fire doors. They'd been waiting for John.

Harvey pulled John back inside and ducked beside the door. He grabbed a large, sharp flat knife from where it hung on the wall. Using the blade as a mirror, he confirmed that he was outnumbered and trapped.

Then he heard the familiar sound of Melody's barking dog. The MP5 had such a unique growl as it spat 5.56mm rounds from its muzzle in bursts of three. Harvey took another glance in the blade. He could just make out the man who'd been firing the AR from his hip now shooting back towards the car park. Harvey pushed John against the wall for him to stay there then made his way outside. He raised his Sig, and took down the man with the AR, then bent to pick up the weapon. Other men had fallen back, and were concentrating fire on Melody. Harvey finished the magazine in short bursts to keep the attackers' heads down. He whistled to John and gestured for them to go. "Where's your car?"

John fumbled for his keys then hit the button on the fob. The lights on a silver Bentley Continental flashed once, and the interior light gracefully grew brighter.

"Let's go," said Harvey.

Melody was fifty feet to Harvey's left, half in and half out of the VW van. Harvey figured she would have her peli-case open beside her with magazines being reloaded and lined up for her by Jackson.

Harvey didn't acknowledge the team. Instead, he opened the passenger door of the Bentley and helped John duck inside. He then climbed into the driver's seat.

Harvey slammed the car into drive, span the wheel and accelerated. The rear end span out almost immediately and the vehicle began to move sideways out the car park. Harvey corrected the over-steer with short, sharp twitches of the wheel. Men stood like rabbits in the headlights as the Bentley lurched towards them. Rifles clanged into the side of the car, metal on metal, and heads bounced off the tempered glass windows, bone on glass.

Sliding the car towards the exit, Harvey quickly span the wheel onto the opposite lock, allowing the rear to skid out noisily onto the tarmac road. Harvey found second gear and held it. The rear wheels span and filled the road with smoke. Gunfire dotted the car's bodywork as the tyres found traction and the massive torque sent the car up to seventy miles per hour in less than four seconds, a long time when men are stood on the road behind firing automatic weapons.

"Where're we going, Harv?" said John, rising up from his ducked position in the car.

"For a drive. Keep your head down."

"They're my guys, Harvey. I can't leave them."

Harvey didn't reply.

"Harv, they're my blokes."

"Not anymore they're not, John," said Harvey coldly. "They weren't prepared. Most of them will be dead by now."

"So much fucking death, Harvey," said John. "I thought the eighties were bad."

Harvey dropped the speed down to fifty to avoid attention from the police then settled into cruise control.

"It's a shame," said John. Harvey glanced across at him. "I liked that club."

"I would've thought you'd prefer something a little more classical?"

"Well, something a little more classy, for sure. But the birds there were always good and willing."

Harvey didn't reply.

"Plus, it used to be Thomson's, which somehow sweetened it for me. Know what I mean, Harv?" John paused. "Where we going anyway?"

"For a walk."

"A walk?" replied John. "It's the middle of the night, and it's November."

"So we'll walk fast."

"The house?"

Harvey didn't reply.

"You've been back, haven't you?"

"A few times."

"I knew you'd bring me here."

"It's nostalgic, John."

"So many happy memories, eh?"

"Just memories, John."

"You know I still own it?"

"I heard you couldn't sell it."

"Yeah, lawyers manage the estate now. Keeps me under the radar. But they do checks on all the assets every six months."

Harvey didn't reply.

"It's funny," began John, "they keep finding bodies there in the basement, where, you know?"

"Sergio, John."

"Yeah, the basement. Must be something that draws people there to off someone."

"Is that right?"

"Cross my heart, Harv. Apparently, last time they found some rag-head down there. No wonder no-one wants to buy it."

Harvey didn't reply. He turned the Bentley's steering wheel and manoeuvred the car through the gates of the old house. The tyres crunched on the gravel, and the headlights cut a bleak path through the gloomy fog that rose from the unkempt, overgrown lawns. The large house stood like a forgotten friend and emerged from the mist as they neared. Two front windows halfway up the two curved staircases inside stared like black eyes in the night. The large wooden double doors hung open like a gaping mouth. Horror, frozen in time.

"Look at the state of the bloody place," said John. "Hard to imagine all the good times we had here, eh?"

Harvey didn't reply.

John climbed out the car and pulled his coat around him. Harvey turned the engine off and followed suit. He stood with his leather biker's jacket flapping in the wind and his white t-shirt glowing in the faint light.

"Shall we have a look around?" asked John, and he began to walk off.

Harvey walked with him to one side, but close enough that they only had to talk quietly. It was like the fog enclosed them in a tiny space, where only they could hear or see each other.

"You were always quiet," said John. "As a kid, you were great fun, but you were always reserved. It was nice. You weren't noisy, not like Donny when he was that age. But I always thought you'd grow out of it."

Harvey glanced across.

John returned the glance and held Harvey's stare. "You never did." He smiled the smile of an old man who'd seen it all and knew that life held few surprises for him anymore.

"They called me, you know," said John, "when they pulled Donny out. I heard mixed stories, none of them pleasant. But I knew you were involved. I'm not sure how, but I just knew."

"What did you hear?"

"He'd killed some young girls, or sold them or something. Something bad."

"Did you know about him and Sergio?"

John paused then said softly, "No. No, I didn't. I was his father, Harvey, but when I heard, I didn't disbelieve it. Not for one second. I knew he was guilty as soon as they told me. I'm so sorry."

"You watched me struggle for all those years?"

"You wouldn't understand."

"I do now. I've had what you might call a moment of clarity, John." Harvey took a lungful of the moist air. "You watched me struggle to find Hannah's killer for all those years, and never helped because deep down you always knew, didn't you?"

John looked at Harvey, pleading with his eyes. "I couldn't change it. The lies had gone too far."

"Tell me where Leo and Olivia are buried."

John stopped in his tracks.

"You see, John, what amazes me is how inhibiting you were. Not only did you fail to tell me who killed Hannah, who killed my parents and why, but you stopped me from finding out, didn't you?"

"No, Harvey, I-"

"Save it, John. I've been away for two years now, and not only have I found the men that killed Hannah, but I also found the man that really killed my parents." They walked on a few steps in silence. "It was there for me all along, John."

"Donny?" said John.

"I watched him die."

"Adeo?"

"He confessed before I killed him."

"So that's you done then, Harvey. You must be happy. That list of yours is all ticked off, and you can go sit on that beach of yours, eh?"

"Not yet, John. I still have a few loose ends to tie up."

"Yeah, I'd like to disappear somewhere hot," said John. "Sit by the pool and fade into old age in style. But..."

"But what?"

"I never could sit still. I'm surprised you can, to be honest."

"I like to read."

"What do you read?"

Harvey gave him a look to ask if they were really now talking about what books they read. "Books. Whatever. Anything that distracts me from reality."

They had completed a slow full circle of the house and stood at the bottom of the few steps that led to the front door.

"So you reckon you're going back to France, do you?" asked John.

"When I'm ready."

"Who are you looking for? What's the holdup?"

"Julios."

"Oh, I see," said John. "He was more of a father to you than I ever was, wasn't he?"

"You both played different roles."

"You mean I paid for everything, and he taught you everything."

"I'm happy, aren't I?"

"I don't know, Harvey. Are you? You've had a face like a

slapped arse for as long as I can remember." John smiled. "I'm sorry it came to this, Harv. I really am."

John raised his handgun and pointed it at Harvey.

———

Park further down the lane, Jackson," said Melody. "We can walk back up. When was your last firearms refresher?"

"It's due again anytime."

"You feel comfortable with a weapon? It's your choice."

"Yeah, sure."

"Good. Denver tied a polycarbonate holster to the underside of your seat. You've been armed all along."

Jackson reached down, found the Sig P226 and pulled it out, smiling. "My choice, eh?"

"Nearly your choice."

Melody pushed the Diemaco's magazine home and chambered a round. She was satisfied with the smooth, well-oiled action and flicked the safety on. Pulling down her night-vision goggles, she stepped from the van, closing the doors quietly.

The grounds of the house spread out all around her. She'd always been impressed by the property, but in the mist and gloom, it had an eerie feeling about it. It held the memories of too much death.

Harvey had told her once how, as a child, he remembered the house being warm and full of the small things that made a home, vases, flowers, pictures, children, parties and the rest. But after Harvey's foster mother, Barb, had left, the house had grown cold. The cook resigned and the house lady began to fade away. Sadness enveloped the old wooden beams. Thick dust lay on the rugs and the window sills. John's office was clean and the bedrooms were clean, but the rest of the house began to fall into disrepair.

Melody and Jackson stepped quietly through the long grass, moving slowly and listening for the deep grumble of men's voices. They heard nothing. It was as if the mist retained the sound within. Melody used her night-vision goggles and found the two men stood at the front of the house. She remained motionless; she was two hundred feet from the big grand entrance. In the green, animated view of the NV goggles, Melody could easily see John's confident but smaller frame against Harvey's rigid and athletic posture. Though she couldn't hear them, the scene didn't look heated. They seemed to be having a normal, calm conversation.

Maybe Harvey had changed his mind. Maybe he couldn't go through with it. There was no shouting. No flailing arms releasing frustration. Just two calm men in control of their emotions. Father and son, almost.

And then John raised his gun.

# END OF AN ERA

JOHN CARTWRIGHT HELD THE SHINY GLOCK TIGHT WITH both hands.

"It didn't have to come to this," said Harvey.

"So why bring me here?"

"I changed my mind. I owe you more than that. You did raise me."

"I thought that we agreed that it was Julios who raised you?"

"Whoever it was, you're the one who fostered me."

John pulled the hammer back on the weapon. "You took away my only son."

Harvey was surprised at the statement. "He *raped* my sister, *your daughter*." He spoke the words with a distaste in his mouth.

"He was sick. There was always something wrong with him, only child stuff, I guess. But he was still my son, and you took him away."

"He was a *monster*. He was bringing girls in from Europe and selling their deaths with sex. It's one of the sickest things I've ever come across, John."

"No Harvey, you're sick. How many sons or fathers or brothers have you taken away?"

Harvey didn't reply.

"Tell me who the monster is *now?*"

"Tell me where they're buried."

"Who? Leo and Olivia?" asked John. He laughed. "They're buried right here, Harvey."

"Here? Under my nose all this time?" said Harvey, stepping towards John. "You gave the order, didn't you? You bloody killed them. All those times I asked you about my parents, and you told me that same old cock and bull story about-"

"Finding the pair of you in a booth in my bar in East Ham. We did everything ourselves back then, you know, even served drinks when the bar staff were busy."

"That's the one," said Harvey. "I was in a hamper."

"It was for your own good, Harvey."

"I was going to let you walk away."

"Then you're dumber than I give you credit for."

"Where?"

"In the orchard."

"Where we used to play?"

"They're not the only ones, Harvey," said John. "You'll be surprised at the secrets this place holds. Plus there's always room for one more in there."

"You're really going to kill me?" Harvey was incredulous. "Of all the people in the world, it boils down to this, does it? Killed by my own foster father."

"You killed Donny. I can't let it go."

"You killed my parents."

"Touché," said John. "You're a cop."

Harvey was stunned. He hadn't been ready for John to know the truth.

"That's right, I know *all* about it. How you left Donny

here for the women to tear him to bits. How you brought Stimson down, and I know all about the terrorist. What was his name, Al Sayan?"

"Who told you about all of this?"

"It doesn't matter, Harvey. The fact is that you turned. You have to understand that, as uncomfortable as it makes me to say this, I can't have a foster son as a copper. Think of the damage it would do. One of us has to go and, as I'm the one with the gun, well..."

Harvey inhaled deeply through his nose and stared down at his foster father.

"I do love you, Son."

Harvey didn't reply.

"I love you enough to complete you before, you know."

"Complete me?"

"Julios, Harvey," said John, "or Edgar Parrish as he was known before he took the rap for his little brother. See Harvey, that's what brothers do for each other, help them, stick up for them. Not leave them in a basement to be torn to pieces."

"You know?"

"Who killed Julios? Of course, I know, Harvey. In case you've forgotten, *I* run the East End. You don't get to sit in *my* chair at *my* desk without knowing a few people in the right places. Even if some of those places are a little *questionable*."

"How did you find out?"

"I know people, Harvey," said John. "You get all sorts of information. Especially when one of your closest friends is shot dead during a gun deal."

"They're not friends, John. They're on your payroll."

"Well this guy is not on my payroll," said John. "But he was close with Terry Thomson before you shot him."

Harvey thought back to the night Julios had been killed. The black Range Rover that had sat in the clearing, watching.

"I wouldn't call him a friend as such, but we've both looked out for you along the way."

"You both?" said Harvey. "Who? Who was it?"

John's face curled into a tight smile. "Frank."

Harvey was winded, dizzied.

"Do you know how much it costs to keep someone like you out of prison, Harvey? Money. Lots of money and lots of friends in high places. So don't make this harder than it already is. You've got your closure. Now turn and look me in the eye."

Harvey turned slowly, still taken back by the shock. Frank. All along, it had been Frank. That's how he'd kept the noose so tight, because he had all the answers. Harvey had been played all this time. The one person left on his list had been stood beside him all along, just as Sergio and Donny had been.

Harvey straightened and turned completely to face John.

"Anything you want to say?"

"No. Just do it." Harvey held his arms out wide.

"Goodbye, Son." John's finger began to squeeze the trigger.

Harvey didn't reply.

Something metallic clicked far off in the mist to John's right. He glanced away momentarily.

Harvey raised his own weapon and aimed it at John's head.

John turned back to Harvey, his own weapon still aimed at his son.

"It's you or me, Harvey," said John.

Harvey squeezed the trigger, but his hand shook.

"You can't do it, can you?"

Harvey breathed through pursed lips, clenched tight against his teeth.

"If you're going to do it, Harvey. Now's the time."

Harvey brought his other hand up to steady the aim, but they both shook visibly. He lowered the gun and stared at John, who strengthened his stance.

"I can't do it," said Harvey.

---

"Shhh, you hear that?" whispered Melody.

Jackson nodded in the dim light and pointed to Melody's ten o'clock. She pulled the night-vision goggles towards her eyes and tracked a lone man creeping silently across the lawn from where Harvey's little groundsman's house stood derelict and graffitied. The man was trained. He moved well and was patient. He reached within one hundred feet of Harvey and John Cartwright then dropped to the ground. It was then that Melody saw the shape of the rifle. The man quietly folded down a bi-pod and moved into prone position, pulling the rifle into his shoulder. Melody flicked back to John and Harvey. Harvey held his hands up like he was welcoming death. John's silhouette aimed the gun like a man who had been around guns. His stance was strong despite his age.

"Who is it?" whispered Jackson.

"I don't know. But we can't disrupt the state of play now."

"Harvey is going to be shot."

"No," said Melody. "He wouldn't let himself get shot."

"He's looking pretty close."

"No," she said. "No, Harvey would at least try." She pulled the scope back to her eye and found the pair of men in the rifle's night-vision scope. John had straightened up. He was ready to fire.

The shadowed figure to their right slid the rifle bolt

home. Melody heard the dull metallic click. She whipped the rifle to her right and saw the man taking aim.

Turning back, she refocused on Cartwright. "Do something, Harvey," she whispered. "Don't just stand there."

Relief washed over Melody as Harvey raised his gun. The two men faced each other, each with pointed weapons.

"Come on, Harvey," she whispered.

Then a sickening feeling clawed her gut as Harvey lowered his gun, and time stood still as John re-aimed his own. Harvey looked defeated. His arms hung limply by his sides. Melody watched like a voyeur. She aimed but begged silently for Harvey to move. Then the silence was shattered by the report of the stranger's rifle.

The green-hued night vision turned bright white as John's hand clenched, pulling the trigger on his handgun. The vision refocused in time for Melody to see John Cartwright drop to the ground. He seemed to fall backwards in slow motion as gravity overcame his body.

Melody snatched at the rifle and aimed at the stranger. She saw as he reloaded and shifted his aim onto Harvey, preparing to shoot once more.

"Harvey, get down!" she screamed.

The man's head popped up and searched the mist for her. Melody saw as his eyes must have found her, and his rifle began to swing around onto her location.

Melody had already aimed. She released the shot. The 7.62mm round rang out clearly in the mist, louder than the other two shots that had fired. The echo seemed to last forever.

She rolled to her feet, bringing the rifle up with her. Jackson followed as she made her way to the stranger she'd just killed.

She stopped and looked at the body of the man who lay on the ground.

"Oh god."

---

Melody and Jackson stood over the body, a dark shape in the mist that rolled across the wild, un-kept lawns of John Cartwright's old house. The body lay face down and still on the butt of the rifle. Jackson used the toe of his boot to raise the man's hip and roll him onto his back. Melody had the man covered should he pull a weapon from underneath him, but he was clearly dead. The side of his head had been ripped apart with the exit of Melody's round.

"Going to be a tough one to explain," said Jackson.

Melody dropped to her knees and fought to hold back her tears. She bent and rested her head on Frank's chest until a sob came from somewhere deep inside her. She didn't know if it was shame, guilt, or the death of a friend and mentor.

"Melody," said Jackson, "let's go."

"You didn't know him," she replied. "Not like I did."

"Melody, he was in up to his eyeballs."

She straightened and turned to face Jackson, who stood over her, unemotional with a hardened face.

"We were watching him," began Jackson, "for months now. He had calls with known suspects and perverted the course of justice to suit his own well-being."

"No, not Frank," said Melody. "He wouldn't-"

"Terry Thomson, Melody. We have audio recordings of the calls."

"But he'd never-"

"But he did, Melody." Jackson's voice softened. "I know it's not easy to hear, but-"

"What do *you* know? Who *are* you?"

"Let's just say that my transfer to Frank's team wasn't a coincidence."

Sirens grew louder in the still night air, and the mist seemed to try to cover the dead with its spreading wispy limbs.

Melody stared down at the body. Frank Carver's emotionless face stared back at her. There was no expression of surprise, anger or hate. Just peace.

"We need to find Stone."

"You don't need to do anything," hissed Melody. "I'll find Harvey."

"He's wanted, Melody."

"He was cleared. You can't. Leave him."

"Who cleared him?"

The question hung in the air.

"Frank."

"You think that's legit?"

"Let me find him. If anyone is going to bring him in, it'll be me."

Jackson nodded faintly.

"Goodbye, Frank," said Melody under her breath before she stepped away and headed to where she truly dreaded to step.

John Cartwright lay flat on his back with his arms outstretched like an extra in a low budget gangster movie. He stared up at the sky with an open mouth held in a grimace. Melody wondered what his last thought had been. He'd been about to kill his son. He'd betrayed his own, something that Melody knew wouldn't sit right with many of the old school firms.

Melody searched the area for Harvey, but he'd gone.

"You've got twenty minutes to find him and bring him in. I won't be able to hold them off any longer," said Jackson.

Melody walked around the spot where Harvey had stood. There were no tracks visible in the darkness, and the stone steps that led to the two large front doors were empty and cold. Melody turned to watch the headlights of two police cars burst into the grounds and follow the gravel driveway to where she and Jackson stood.

"What's that?" asked Jackson.

Melody followed his gaze to the house. A dim light came from inside. It was soft at first, but by the time the police had found them in the fog, the dim light had turned to a flickering flame. Just briefly, at the rear of the house where the stairs of the basement opened out into the kitchen, Melody thought she saw the shape of a man. Harvey. He stood there facing her, motionless as the fire grew, then vanished.

"Harvey," Melody called out. "Harvey, it's over."

Harvey didn't reply.

The small fire grew into a hungry blaze that chewed through the ancient wooden house, consuming its secrets of the past. Before long, the glow and heat of the fire held the mist at bay, and the spinning blue lights of police cars, ambulances and fire engines lit a riot of chaos and colour in the night.

The thump of helicopter blades suddenly became audible over the growing noise of the fire.

"Go find him, Melody," said Jackson. "I'll hold them off as long as I can."

Melody sprinted into the mist to the rear of the house. The large empty pool lay like an animal trap in the poor light, and the weathered outbuildings looked sad and derelict in the glow of the fire. She caught sight of movement ahead on the tree line. It was Harvey. It was as if he was waiting for her to spot him before he disappeared into the trees.

Small branches gave way as she burst into the orchard. Lines of trees that had once been well maintained were now overgrown with plants and trees that fought for light. She stopped, looked and listened. It was silent inside the orchard. Only the faint trickle of a stream could be heard.

"I guess I owe you thanks," said Harvey.

Melody turned and found him stood beside a tree.

"No," she said. "No thanks needed."

"You saved my life again."

"You would have done the same."

"Was it Frank?"

"What makes you think that?"

"Was it Frank, Melody?"

"Yes," she said, her voice at breaking point.

"I always thought he was dirty. John confirmed it."

"Don't say that. He saved you."

"He saved himself, Melody, or tried to, at least. He was on terms with John and Terry Thomson. He knew all along who killed Julios."

"It was Frank, wasn't it?"

Harvey didn't reply.

"Are you coming easy?"

Harvey sighed audibly. "Am I being arrested?"

"It's Jackson," began Melody. "He was onto Frank. He's holding them off, so if you come quietly-"

"If I come quietly, there'll be no fuss, is that right?"

"Don't make this hard, Harvey."

"Hannah and I used to play here as kids."

"It's nice. You were lucky."

Harvey laughed. "Lucky, eh?"

"Privileged?"

"Closer, I guess. I was for a while anyway," said Harvey. "They're buried here, you know?"

Melody looked at him in the darkness. "Do you feel closure, Harvey?"

"Closure?"

"You found the answers you were looking for. Do you feel like you can rest now?"

"In prison, you mean?"

"It doesn't have to go that way, Harvey. Think of all the good things you've done with us. That has to stand for something."

"Think of all the bad things I've done along the way, Melody."

"You're not a bad person, Harvey."

Harvey didn't reply.

"Come with me. I can make sure they go easy on you."

"Take care of yourself, Melody."

A huge fireball lit the scene behind Melody as the roof of the great house caved in, and the blaze reached up for the cool air. Melody span around and watched the spectacle.

"That's the end of an era, Harvey."

Harvey didn't reply.

"There's a lot of memories going up in flames."

Harvey didn't reply.

"Harvey?"

Melody searched the darkness. The space where he had leant against the tree was empty. No movement caught her eye.

Harvey was gone.

## DEBRIEF

MELODY STOOD AT THE HEAD OF THE MESS ROOM WHERE Frank used to stand. Reg sat on the couch where he always sat and Jackson perched on the arm of the other chair. Boon sat obediently at Melody's feet, and leaning against the wall beside the door where Harvey used to stand was the chief.

Melody glanced over to the chief and he answered her unspoken question with a gentle nod. She turned to face Reg and Jackson then sat on the edge of the table.

"Our brief was to reduce the growing violence among the territorial gangs in the East End. Namely, to bring the Albanian's spread to a halt." Melody looked up at the ceiling, unable to hold Reg's gaze for any length of time. "I think we can safely say we achieved that. Luan Duri is down, and most of his men are either dead or on the run. Many are believed to have escaped the UK borders." She turned to the chief. "We have eyes on the remainder of the Albanian firm and will make sure they do not try to spread their wings." Melody reached back and hit a key on her laptop. The large screen mounted on a mobile TV stand came to life, and Luan Duri's face appeared upon it.

The chief nodded his approval.

Melody hit the right-hand cursor on the laptop, and Bobby Bones' photo appeared. "During the operation," Melody continued, "Robert Carnell, AKA Bobby 'Bones' Carnell, was believed to have been shot dead by members of John Cartwright's firm. Dominic Fox is believed to have taken over Carnell's operations but has been pushed out to North London, Highbury, to be precise. We have eyes on him to make sure he stays there, and the profiles of all known associates have been passed on to the Organised Crime Division."

"Good, Mills," said the chief, and waited for her to continue.

"Now, let's move onto John Cartwright, father of Donald Cartwright, who was recently killed in a human trafficking operation. John has been on the watch list of the Organised Crime Division and its predecessor organisations such as SO10 and SOCA for more than forty years. He was taken down by the very man that kept him out of our reach, the same man that diverted our attention and ensured that John Cartwright's very existence was in the shadows." Melody hit the right-hand arrow on the laptop's keyboard one last time and Reg gasped at the image.

"Frank Carver has been under surveillance of the Organised Crime Division and internal affairs for two years." Melody paused to allow her throat to open itself and for her emotions to calm. She took a deep breath. "Frank Carver was guilty of perverting the course of justice and was responsible for at least one murder." She paused. "Edgar Parrish, AKA Julios." Melody stared directly at Reg who sat aghast at the news. "I recently received confirmation that Carver was the killer."

Melody turned back to the chief. "I'd call this operation a huge success."

Reg began a small clap at Melody's debrief. It was in jest, but Jackson joined in, and the chief added three small claps before pushing himself off the wall. Reg and Jackson stopped and stood. Boon walked beside them as they left the room. As Melody stepped in behind them, the chief held his hand out to stop her.

"Stay, Mills. There's something I'd like to discuss."

# BEACH

HARVEY STONE LAY ON THE EDGE OF A LONG GOLDEN beach in the small town of Argelles in the south of France. The empty beach stretched out before him, and long grass blew in the soft breeze behind him. It was midday and the heat was at its peak. He lay with a book by his side, closed neatly with a ten-euro note to mark the page. His eyes were closed to the bright sun but its rays brought life to his skin, and the soft, cool breeze cleansed his body of old memories.

He felt the sun fall into shadow on his eyelids.

"You're in my light."

"I am the light."

"Are you? Any danger you could shine somewhere else?"

"You're a hard man to find," said the woman.

"I'm not exactly hiding."

"I followed you all the way from Essex."

"I wasn't exactly running either."

Harvey felt the woman step around him then watched her in his mind as she stood gazing out to sea.

"How do we do this, Harvey?"

"How do we do what? It's the end, isn't it?"

"It doesn't have to be."

Harvey didn't reply.

"I could use a man like you."

"Someone who doesn't mind getting his hands dirty?"

"Among other things."

"I thought they were already dirty? Are you bringing me in?"

"Not necessarily."

Harvey opened his eyes and craned his neck forward to see Melody stood silhouetted by the sun. Her hair blew softly in the breeze and rested on her shoulders, and her short leather jacket flapped against her side.

"Two choices," she said.

"Let me guess, one bad, one worse."

"I wouldn't say that."

"Well, what then? I'm a busy man, can't you see?"

"First choice, you come back to London with me. The chief offered me Frank's job. I can have you cleared as an operative, you know."

"I'd report to you?"

"You always did, really."

"Second choice?"

Melody dropped slowly to her knees, leaned forward onto all fours and crawled up Harvey's body. Her eyes fixed on Harvey's. She stopped inches from his face.

"This," she said, and kissed him.

Harvey didn't reply.

# A NOTE FROM THE AUTHOR

The back streets of Silvertown and Canning Town are a buzzing place to be. A blend of old and new build housing alongside the industrial bank of the Thames provided me with plenty of canvass with which to bring Harvey back to the gangland world he's so very much a part of.

The pubs in Stone Rage were all based on memories of pubs I remembered, but with different names, and the people were based loosely on some of the colorful characters I met during my time in the area.

The house in Theydon Bois, was of course where my parents once lived and I thought it a suitable ending to this particular chapter of Harvey's life. I hope you did too.

So onward and upward, a new set of Stone Cold Thrillers is waiting for you. If you've reached this far, I think you're going to love where Harvey is going...

Thank you for reading.

J.D. Weston

*To learn more about J.D. Weston*

www.jdweston.com

john@jdweston.com

# ALSO BY J.D.WESTON.

## The Stone Cold Thriller Series.

Book 1 - Stone Cold.

Book 2 - Stone Fury

Book 3 - Stone Fall

Book 4 - Stone Rage

Book 5 - Stone Free

Book 6 - Stone Rush

Book 7 - Stone Game

Book 8 - Stone Raid

Book 9 - Stone Deep

Book 10 - Stone Fist

## Novellas

Stone Breed

Stone Blood

## The Alaskan Adventure

Where the Mountains Kiss the Sun

From the Ocean to the Stream

.

# STONE COLD

### Book One of the Stone Cold Thriller series

**One priceless set of diamonds. Three of London's ruthless east end crime families. One very angry assassin with a hit list.**

Harvey Stone has questions that someone will answer. Who killed his parents and why? Who raped and killed his sister? And why are his closest allies hiding the truth.

When Harvey is asked to kill east London's biggest crime boss in return for one name on his list, there is only one answer.

Can Harvey survive the gang war, untangle the web of deceit and uncover the truth behind his sisters death?

Stone Cold is the first book in the Stone Cold thriller series.

If you enjoy fast-paced adventure, gritty vigilante stories and no-nonsense heroes, then you'll love J.D. Weston's brand new Thriller Series.

## STONE FURY

### Book Two of the Stone Cold Thriller series

**The lives of twelve young girls are being sold. The seller is on Harvey Stone's hit list.**

When ex-hitman Harvey Stone learns of an human trafficking ring taking place in his old stomping ground, he is sickened. But when he learns the name of the person running the show, an opportunity arises to cross one more name of his list.

Can Harvey save the ill-fated girls, and serve justice to those who are most deserved?

Stone Fury is the second book in the Stone Cold thriller series.

If you enjoy fast-paced adventure, gritty vigilante stories and no-nonsense heroes, then you'll love J.D. Weston's brand new Thriller Series.

# STONE FALL

## Book Three of the Stone Cold Thriller series

**One evil terrorist with a plan to change the face of London. One missing child, and one priceless jade Buddha. Only Harvey Stone and his team of organised crime specialists can prevent disaster.**

When Harvey and the team intercept a heist to rob a priceless jade Buddha, little did they know they would be uncovering a terrorist attack on London's St Paul's Cathedral, and a shocking hostage scenario.

Can Harvey and the team stop the terrorists, save the little girl and rescue the priceless Buddha?

Stone Fall is the third book in the Stone Cold thriller series.

If you enjoy fast-paced adventure, gritty vigilante stories and no-nonsense heroes, then you'll love J.D. Weston's brand new Thriller Series.

## STONE RAGE

### Book Four of the Stone Cold Thriller series

**Two of east London's most notorious gangs go head to
head with the Albanian mafia, and one angry assassin
who's out to clean up.**
When Harvey Stone is sent undercover to put a stop a turf
war between the Albanian mafia and two of East London's
most notorious gangs, nobody expected him to be welcomed
like a hero by an old face.

Has Harvey finally gone rogue, or will he put a stop to the
bloodshed once and for all?

Stone Rage is the fourth book in the Stone Cold thriller
series.
If you enjoy fast-paced adventure, gritty vigilante stories and
no-nonsense heroes, then you'll love J.D.Weston's brand new
Thriller Series.

## STONE FREE

### Book Five of the Stone Cold Thriller series

**Death by internet. A mind blowing masterplan, where death holds all the cards.**

Harvey Stone plays guardian angel on international soil when two governments prepare to do battle, and the lives of innocent people are at stake.

Can Harvey free the condemned women and avert an international disaster. Can he defy all odds and escape alive?

Find out in Stone Free, the fifth book in the Stone Cold Thriller series.

If you enjoy intense thrillers, with shocking storylines, then you'll love this new series from J.D. Weston.

## STONE RUSH

### Book Six of the Stone Cold Thriller series

**Europe's slave trade is alive. MI6 is falling down, and Harvey Stone is caught in the middle.**

Harvey yearns for the quiet life, but when a close friend is captured and tortured, and refugees become slaves, Harvey is forced out of retirement.

Can Harvey put a stop to the human traffickers and save the girls from a torturous death? Can he prevent the gang's devastating plans?

Find out, in Stone Rush, the sixth book in the Stone Cold Thriller series.

If you enjoy intense thrillers, with shocking storylines, then you'll love this new action crime thriller from J.D. Weston.

# STONE GAME

## Book Seven of the Stone Cold Thriller series

**Tragedy strikes. A killer runs wild, and an old enemy raises the stakes.**

Memories of Harvey's kills return to haunt his freedom. But as the body count grows and the past become reality, the hunter becomes the hunted.

Has Harvey gone back to his old ways? Is he destined for a life on the run?

Stone Game is the seventh book in J.D. Weston's Stone Cold Thriller series.

If you like your action hard and fast, with page-turning intensity, you'll love this series.

# STONE RAID

## Book Eight of the Stone Cold Thriller series

**A pair of cursed diamonds. A brutal gang ran by evil twin brothers. And an ex-hitman who finds himself deep inside a Victorian legend.**

When ex-hitman Harvey Stone emerges from laying low, he stumbles into a cruel and twisted plot devised by evil twin brothers to bring together two cursed diamonds, and unleash hell in London.

But the deeper Harvey delves into their plans, the more twisted they become, and saving the diamonds becomes his toughest challenge yet.

Can Harvey bring down the evil twins and prevent the cursed diamonds from destroying more lives? Can he find right from wrong in this twisted tale of lies and deceit?

# STONE DEEP

## Book Nine of the Stone Cold Thriller series

**An ancient Spanish legacy. A shocking explosion in the City of London. And an ex-hitman fueled by revenge.**

When ex-hitman, Harvey Stone is asked by an art collector, Smokey the Jew, to kidnap a member of a rival gang and extract details of a heist, little did he know the move would open the doors of hell and endanger everyone he cares for.

But renowned art thief, Dante Dumas will go to any length to find his family legacy, killing anyone who stands in his way.

Can Harvey survive Dante's devious plans, and can he find retribution for his lost love?

# STONE FIST

## Book Ten of the Stone Cold Thriller series

**Two East London gangs. One ex-hitman clinging to the past. And a brutal fight to the death.**

When ex-hitman Harvey Stone visits London to attend the wedding of one of his closest allies, he plans a visit to the grave of his long-dead mentor, Julios. But little does Harvey know that the trip will uncover a secret that will change his life forever and open doors to Harvey's past that have never before been revealed. But to forge an allegiance with a blast from Harvey's past he must first deal with a brutal death match between two rival gangs that threatens to wipe history from the face of the earth before it's even exposed.

# ACKNOWLEDGMENTS

Authors are often portrayed as having very lonely work lives. There breeds a stereotypical image of reclusive authors talking only to their cat or dog and their editor, and living off cereal and brandy.

I beg to differ.

There is absolutely no way on the planet that this book could have been created to the standard it is without the help and support of Erica Bawden, Paul Weston, Danny Maguire, and Heather Draper. All of whom offered vital feedback during various drafts and supported me while I locked myself away and spoke to my imaginary dog, ate cereal and drank brandy.

The book was painstakingly edited by Ceri Savage, who continues to sit with me on Skype every week as we flesh out the series, and also threw in some amazing ideas.

To those named above, I am truly grateful.

J.D. Weston.